I0677469

TOURNAMENT UNDER NIGHTMARE SKIES

When Kit Temple was drafted for the Nowhere Journey, he figured that he'd left his home, his girl, and the Earth for good. For though those called were always promised "rotation," not a man had ever returned from that mysterious flight into the unknown.

Kit's fellow-draftee Arkalion, the young man with the strange, old-man eyes, seemed to know more than he should. So when Kit twisted the tail of fate and followed Arkalion to the ends of space and time, he found the secret behind "Nowhere" and a personal challenge upon which the entire future of Earth depended.

———————

MILTON LESSER started reading science-fiction in 1939, and began writing it in 1949. Since then he has had a myriad stories and novels published under many pen-names. Of this novel, he writes:

"Along with a lot of other people, I like to write about the first interstellar voyage. The reason is simple. Once mankind gets out to the stars and begins to spread out across the galaxy, he'll be immortal despite his best—make that *worst*—efforts to destroy himself. You can destroy a world, maybe a dozen worlds, but spread humanity out thin among the stars, colonies here, there, and all over, and he's immortal. He'll live as long as there's a universe to hold him.

"I know interstellar travel is a long way off, but science has a way of leaping ahead in geometric, not arithmetic progression. A hundred years? Perhaps we'll have our first starship then. Let's hope so. For if man can survive the next hundred years—the hardest hundred, I believe—he'll reach the stars and go on forever."

Recruit for Andromeda

by
MILTON LESSER

WILDSIDE PRESS

RECRUIT FOR ANDROMEDA

Copyright ©, 1959, by Ace Books, Inc.

All Rights Reserved

CHAPTER I

WHEN THE FIRST strong sunlight of May covered the tree-arched avenues of Center City with green, the riots started.

The people gathered in angry knots outside the city hall, met in the park and littered its walks with newspapers and magazines as they gobbled up editorial comment at a furious rate, slipped with dark of night through back alleys and planned things with furious futility. Center City's finest knew when to make themselves scarce: their uniforms stood for everything objectionable at this time and they might be subjected to clubs, stones, taunts, threats, leers—and knives.

But Center City, like most communities in United North America, had survived the Riots before and would survive them again. On past performances, the damage could be estimated, too. Two-hundred fifty-seven plate glass windows would be broken, three-hundred twelve limbs fractured. Several thousand people would be treated for minor bruises and abrasions, Center City would receive half that many damage suits. The list had been drawn clearly and accurately; it hardly ever deviated.

And Center City would meet its quota. With a demonstration of reluctance, of course. The healthy approved way to get over social trauma once every seven-hundred eighty days.

"Shut it off, Kit. Kit, please."

The telio blared in a cheaply feminine voice, "Oh, it's a

long way to nowhere, forever. And your honey's not coming back, never, never, never . . ." A wailing trumpet represented flight.

"They'll exploit anything, Kit."

"It's just a song."

"Turn it off, please."

Christopher Temple turned off the telio, smiling. "They'll announce the names in ten minutes," he said, and felt the corners of his mouth draw taut.

"Tell me again, Kit," Stephanie pleaded. "How old are you?"

"You know I'm twenty-six."

"Twenty-six. Yes, twenty-six, so if they don't call you this time, you'll be safe. Safe, I can hardly believe it."

"Nine minutes," said Temple in the darkness. Stephanie had drawn the blinds earlier, had dialed for sound-proofing. The screaming in the streets came to them as not the faintest whisper. But the song which became briefly, masochistically popular every two years and two months had spoiled their feeling of seclusion.

"Tell me again, Kit."

"What."

"You know what."

He let her come to him, let her hug him fiercely and whimper against his chest. He remained passive although it hurt, occasionally stroking her hair. He could not assert himself for another—he looked at his strap chrono—for another eight minutes. He might regret it, if he did, for a lifetime.

"Tell me, Kit."

"I'll marry you, Steffy. In eight minutes, less than eight minutes, I'll go down and get the license. We'll marry as soon as it's legal."

"This is the last time they have a chance for you. I mean, they won't change the law?"

Temple shook his head. "They don't have to. They meet their quota this way."

"I'm scared."

"You and everyone else in North America, Steffy."

She was trembling against him. "It's cold for June."

"It's warm in here." He kissed her moist eyes, her nose, her lips.

"Oh God, Kit. Five minutes."

"Five minutes to freedom," he said jauntily. He did not feel that way at all. Apprehension clutched at his chest with tight, painful fingers, almost making it difficult for him to breathe.

"Turn it on, Kit."

He dialed the telio in time to see the announcer's insincere smile. Smile seventeen, Kit thought wryly. Patriotic sacrifice.

"Every seven-hundred eighty days," said the announcer, "two-hundred of Center City's young men are selected to serve their country for an indeterminate period regulated rigidly by a rotation system."

"Liar!" Stephanie cried. "No one ever comes back. It's been thirty years since the first group and not one of them . . ."

"Shh," Temple raised a finger to his lips.

"This is the thirteenth call since the inception of what is popularly referred to as the Nowhere Journey," said the announcer. "Obviously, the two hundred young men from Center City and the thousands from all over this hemisphere do not in reality embark on a Journey to Nowhere. That is quite meaningless."

"Hooray for him," Temple laughed.

"I wish he'd get on with it."

"No, ladies and gentlemen, we use the word Nowhere merely because we are not aware of the ultimate destination. Security reasons make it impossible to . . ."

"Yes, yes," said Stephanie impatiently. "Go on."

". . . therefore, the Nowhere Journey. With a maximum security lid on the whole project, we don't even know why our men are sent, or by what means. We know only that they go somewhere and not nowhere, bravely and not fearfully, for a purpose vital to the security of this nation and not to slake the thirst of a chessman of regiments and divisions.

"If Center City's contribution helps keep our country strong, Center City is naturally obligated . . ."

"No one ever said it isn't our duty," Stephanie argued, as if the announcer could indeed hear her. "We only wish we knew something about it—and we wish it weren't forever."

"It isn't forever," Temple reminded her. "Not officially."

"Officially, my foot. If they never return, they never return. If there's a rotation system on paper, but it's never used, that's not a rotation system at all. Kit, it's forever."

". . . to thank the following sponsors for relinquishing their time . . ."

"No one would want to sponsor *that*," Temple whispered cheerfully.

"Kit," said Stephanie, "I—I suddenly have a hunch we have nothing to worry about. They missed you all along and they'll miss you this time, too. The last time, and then you'll be too old. That's funny, too old at twenty-six. But we'll be free, Kit. Free."

"He's starting," Temple told her.

A large drum filled the entire telio screen. It rotated slowly from bottom to top. In twenty seconds, the letter A appeared, followed by about a dozen names. Abercrombie, Harold. Abner, Eugene. Adams, Gerald. Sorrow in the Abercrombie household. Despair for the Abners. Black horror for Adams.

The drum rotated.

"They're up to F, Kit."

Fabian, Gregory G . . .

Names circled the drum slowly, live viscous alphabet soup. Meaningless, unless you happened to know them.

"Kit, I knew Thomas Mulvany."

N, O, P . . .

"It's hot in here."

"I thought you were cold."

"I'm suffocating now."

R, S . . .

"T!" Stephanie shrieked as the names began to float slowly up from the bottom of the drum.

Tabor, Tebbets, Teddley . . .

Temple's mouth felt dry as a ball of cotton. Stephanie laughed nervously. Now—or never. Never?

Now.

Stephanie whimpered despairingly.

TEMPLE, CHRISTOPHER.

"Sorry I'm late, Mr. Jones."

"Hardly, Mr. Smith. Hardly. Three minutes late."

"I've come in response to your ad."

"I know. You look old."

"I am over twenty-six. Do you mind?"

"Not if you don't, Mr. Smith. Let me look at you. Umm, you seem the right height, the right build."

"I meet the specifications exactly."

"Good, Mr. Smith. And your price."

"No haggling," said Smith. "I have a price which must be met."

"Your price, Mr. Smith?"

"Ten million dollars."

The man called Jones coughed nervously. "That's high."

"Very. Take it or leave it."

"In cash?"

"Definitely. Small unmarked bills."

"You'd need a moving van!"

"Then I'll get one."

"Ten million dollars," said Jones, "is quite a price. Admittedly, I haven't dealt in this sort of traffic before, but—"

"But nothing. Were your name Jones, really and truly Jones, I might ask less."

"Sir?"

"You are Jones exactly as much as I am Smith."

"Sir?" Jones gasped again.

Smith coughed discreetly. "But I have one advantage. I know you. You don't know me, Mr. Arkalion."

"Eh? Eh?"

"Arkalion. The North American Carpet King. Right?"

"How did you know?" the man whose name was not Jones but Arkalion asked the man whose name was not Smith but might as well have been.

"When I saw your ad," said not-Smith, "I said to myself, 'now here must be a very rich, influential man.' It only remained for me to study a series of photographs readily obtainable—I have a fine memory for that, Mr. Arkalion— and here you are; here is Arkalion the Carpet King."

"What will you do with the ten million dollars?" demanded Arkalion, not minding the loss nearly so much as the ultimate disposition of his fortune.

"Why, what does anyone do with ten million dollars? Treasure it. Invest it. Spend it."

"I mean, what will you do with it if you are going in place of my—" Arkalion bit his tongue.

"Your son, were you saying, Mr. Arkalion? Alaric Arkalion the Third. Did you know that I was able to boil my list of men down to thirty when I studied their family ties?"

"Brilliant, Mr. Smith. Alaric is so young—"

"Aren't they all? Twenty-one to twenty-six. Who was it who once said something about the flower of our young manhood?"

"Shakespeare?" said Mr. Arkalion realizing that most quotes of lasting importance came from the bard.

"Sophocles," said Smith. "But no matter. I will take young Alaric's place for ten million dollars."

Motives always troubled Mr. Arkalion, and thus he pursued what might have been a dangerous conversation. "You'll never get a chance to spend it on the Nowhere Journey."

"Let me worry about that."

"No one ever returns."

"My worry, not yours."

"It is forever—as if you dropped out of existence. Alaric is so young."

"I have always gambled, Mr. Arkalion. If I do not return in five years, you are to put the money in a trust fund for certain designated individuals, said fund to be terminated the moment I return. If I come back within the five years, you are merely to give the money over to me. Is that clear?"

"Yes."

"I'll want it in writing, of course."

"Of course. A plastic surgeon is due here in about ten minutes, Mr. Smith, and we can get on with . . . But if I don't know your name, how can I put it in writing?"

Smith smiled. "I changed my name to Smith for the occasion. Perfectly legal. My name is John X. Smith—now!"

"That's where you're wrong," said Mr. Arkalion as the plastic surgeon entered. "Your name is Alaric Arkalion III—now."

The plastic surgeon skittered around Smith, examining him minutely with the casual expertness that comes with experience.

"Have to shorten the cheek bones."

"For ten million dollars," said Smith, "you can take the damned things out altogether and hang them on your wall."

Sophia Androvna Petrovitch made her way downtown

through the bustle of tired workers and the occasional sprinkling of Comrades. She crushed her *ersatz* cigarette underfoot at number 616 Stalin Avenue, paused for the space of five heartbeats at the door, went inside.

"What do you want?" The man at the desk was myopic but bull-necked.

Sophia showed her party card.

"Oh, Comrade. Still, you are a woman."

"You're terribly observant, Comrade," said Sophia coldly. "I am here to volunteer."

"But a woman."

"There is nothing in the law which says a woman cannot volunteer."

"We don't make women volunteer."

"I mean really volunteer, of her own free will."

"Her—own—free will?" The bull-necked man removed his spectacles, scratched his balding head with the ear-pieces. "You mean volunteer without—"

"Without coercion. I want to volunteer. I am here to volunteer. I want to sign on for the next Stalintrek."

"Stalintrek, a woman?"

"That is what I said."

"We don't force women to volunteer." The man scratched some more.

"Oh, really," said Sophia. "This is 1992, not mid-century, Comrade. Did not Stalin say, 'Woman was created to share the glorious destiny of Mother Russia with her mate?'" Sophia created the quote randomly.

"Yes, if Stalin said—"

"He did."

"Still, I do not recall—"

"What?" Sophia cried. "Stalin dead these thirty-nine years and you don't recall his speeches? What is your name, Comrade?"

"Please, Comrade. Now that you remind me, I remember."

"What is your name."

"Here, I will give you the volunteer papers to sign. If you pass the exams, you will embark on the next Stalintrek, though why a beautiful young woman like you—"

"Shut your mouth and hand me those papers."

There, sitting behind that desk, was precisely why. Why should she, Sophia Androvna Petrovich, wish to volunteer for the Stalintrek? Better to ask why a bird flies south in the winter, one day ahead of the first icy gale. Or why a lemming plunges recklessly into the sea with his multitudes of fellows, if, indeed, the venture were to turn out grimly.

But there, behind that desk, was part of the reason. The Comrade. The bright sharp Comrade, with his depth of reasoning, his fountain of gushing emotions, his worldliness. *Pfooey!*

It was as if she had been in a cocoon all her life, stifled, starved, the cottony inner lining choking her whenever she opened her mouth, the leathery outer covering restricting her when she tried to move. No one had ever returned from the Stalintrek. She then had to assume no one would. Including Sophia Androvna Petrovitch. But then, there was nothing she would miss, nothing to which she particularly wanted to return. Not the stark, foul streets of Stalingrad, not the workers with their vapid faces or the Comrades with their cautious, sweating, trembling, fearful non-decisions, not the higher echelon of Comrades, more frightened but showing it less, who would love the beauty of her breasts and loins but not herself for you never love anything but the Stalinimage and Mother Russia herself, not those terrified martinet-marionettes who would love the parts of her if she permitted but not her or any other person for that matter.

Wrong with the Stalintrek was its name alone, a name one associated with everything else in Russia for an obvious, post-Stalin reason. But everything else about the Stalintrek shrieked mystery and adventure. Where did you go? How did you get there? What did you do? Why?

A million questions which had kept her awake at night and, if she thought about them hard enough, satisfied her deep longing for something different. And then one day when stolid Mrs. Ivanovna-Rasnikov had said, "It is a joke, a terrible, terrible joke they are taking my husband Fyodor on the Stalintrek when he lacks sufficient imagination to go from here to Leningrad or even Tula. Can you picture Fyodor on the Stalintrek? Better they should have taken me. Better they should have taken his wife." That day Sophia could hardly contain herself.

As a party member she had access to the law and she read it three times from start to finish (in her dingy flat by the light of a smoking, foul-smelling, soft-wax candle) but could find nothing barring women from the Stalintrek.

Had Fyodor Rasnikov volunteered? Naturally. Everyone volunteered, although when your name was called you had no choice. There had been no draft in Russia since the days of the Second War of the People's Liberation. Volunteer? What, precisely, did the word mean?

She, Sophia Androvna Petrovitch would volunteer, without being told. Thus it was she found herself at 616 Stalin Avenue, and thus the balding, myopic, bull-necked Comrade thrust the papers across his desk at her.

She signed her name with such vehemence and ferocity that she almost tore through the paper.

CHAPTER II

*Three-score men sit in the crowded, smoke-filled room.
Some drink beer, some squat in moody silence, some talk in
an animated fashion about nothing very urgent. At the one
small door, two guards pace back and forth slowly, creating
a gentle swaying of smoke-patterns in the hazy room. The
guards, in simple military uniform, carry small, deadly looking weapons.*

FIRST MAN: Fight City Hall? Are you kidding? They
took you, bud. Don't try to fight it, I know. I *know.*

SECOND MAN: I'm telling you, there was a mistake in
the records. I'm over twenty-six. Two weeks and two days.
Already I wrote to my Congressman. Hell, that's why I voted
for him, he better go to bat for me.

THIRD MAN: You think that's something? I wouldn't be
here only those doctors are crazy. I mean, crazy. Me, with
a cyst big as a golf ball on the base of my spine.

FIRST MAN: You too. Don't try to fight it.

FOURTH MAN: (Newly named Alaric Arkalion III) I look
forward to this as a stimulating adventure. Does the fact
that they select men for the Nowhere Journey once every
seven hundred and eighty days strike anyone as significant?

SECOND MAN: I got my own problems.

ALARIC ARKALION: This is not a thalamic problem, young
man. Not thalamic at all.

THIRD MAN: Young man? Who are you kidding?

ALARIC ARKALION: (Who realizes, thanks to the plastic
surgeon, he is the youngest looking of all, with red cheeks
and peachfuzz whiskers) It is a problem of the intellect.
Why seven hundred and eighty days?

FIRST MAN: I read the magazine, too, chief. You think we're all going to the planet Mars. How original.

ALARIC ARKALION: As a matter of fact, that is exactly what I think.

SECOND MAN: Mars?

FIRST MAN: (Laughing) It's a long way from Mars to City Hall, doc.

SECOND MAN: You mean, through space to Mars?

ALARIC ARKALION: Exactly, exactly. Quite a coincidence, otherwise.

FIRST MAN: You're telling me.

ALARIC ARKALION: (Coldly) Would you care to explain it?

FIRST MAN: Why, sure. You see, Mars is—uh, I don't want to steal your thunder, chief. Go ahead.

ALARIC ARKALION: Once every seven hundred and eighty days Mars and the Earth find themselves in the same orbital position with respect to the sun. In other words, Mars and Earth are closest then. Were there such a thing as space travel, new, costly, not thoroughly tested, they would want to make each journey as brief as possible. Hence the seven hundred and eighty days.

FIRST MAN: Not bad, chief. You got most of it.

THIRD MAN: No one ever said anything about space travel.

FIRST MAN: You think we'd broadcast it or something, stupid? It's part of a big, important scientific experiment, only we're the hamsters.

ALARIC ARKALION: Ridiculous. You're forgetting all about the Cold War.

FIRST MAN: He thinks we're fighting a war with the Martians. (Laughs) Orson Wells stuff, huh?

ALARIC ARKALION: With the Russians. The Russians. We developed A bombs. They developed A bombs. We came up with the H bomb. So did they. We placed a station up in

space, a fifth of the way to the moon. So did they. Then
—nothing more about scientific developments. For over
twenty years. I ask you, doesn't it seem peculiar?

FIRST MAN: Peculiar, he says.

ALARIC ARKALION: Peculiar.

SECOND MAN: I wish my Congressman . . .

FIRST MAN: You and your Congressman. The way you talk,
it was your vote got him in office.

SECOND MAN: If only I could get out and talk to him.

ALARIC ARKALION: No one is permitted to leave.

FIRST MAN: Punishable by a prison term, the law says.

SECOND MAN: Oh yeah? Prison, shmision. Or else go on
the Nowhere Journey. Well, I don't see the difference.

FIRST MAN: So, go ahead. Try to escape.

SECOND MAN: (Looking at the guards) They got them all
over. All over. I think our mail is censored.

ALARIC ARKALION: It is.

SECOND MAN: They better watch out. I'm losing my temper. I get violent when I lose my temper.

FIRST MAN: See? See how the guards are trembling.

SECOND MAN: Very funny. Maybe you didn't have a
good job or something? Maybe you don't care. I care. I had
a job with a future. Didn't pay much, but a real blue chip
future. So they send me to Nowhere.

FIRST MAN: You're not there yet.

SECOND MAN: Yeah, but I'm going.

THIRD MAN: If only they let you know when. My back is
killing me. I'm waiting to pull a sick act. Just waiting, that's
all.

FIRST MAN: Go ahead and wait, a lot of good it will do
you.

THIRD MAN: You mind your own business.

FIRST MAN: I am, doc. You brought the whole thing up.

SECOND MAN: He's looking for trouble.

THIRD MAN: He'll get it.

ALARIC ARKALION: We're going to be together a long time. A long time. Why don't you all relax?

SECOND MAN: You mind your own business.

FIRST MAN: Nuts, aren't they. They're nuts. A sick act, yet.

SECOND MAN: Look how it doesn't bother him. A failure, he was. I can just see it. What does he care if he goes away forever and doesn't come back? One bread line is as good as another.

FIRST MAN: Ha-ha.

SECOND MAN: Yeah, well I mean it. Forever. We're going away, someplace—forever. We're not coming back, ever. No one comes back. It's for good, for keeps.

FIRST MAN: Tell it to your congressman. Or maybe you want to pull a sick act, too?

THIRD MAN: (Hits First Man, who, surprised, crashes back against a table and falls down) It isn't an act, damn you!

GUARD: All right, break it up. Come on, break it up . . .

ALARIC ARKALION: (To himself) I wish I saw that ten million dollars already—*if* I ever get to see it.

They drove for hours through the fresh country air, feeling the wind against their faces, listening to the roar their ground-jet made, all alone on the rimrock highway.

"Where are we going, Kit?"

"Search me. Just driving."

"I'm glad they let you come out this once. I don't know what they would have done to me if they didn't. I had to see you this once. I—"

Temple smiled. He had absented himself without leave. It had been difficult enough and he might yet be in a lot of hot water, but it would be senseless to worry Stephanie. "It's just for a few hours," he said.

"Hours. When we want a whole lifetime. Kit. Oh, Kit—why don't we run away? Just the two of us, someplace where they'll never find you. I could be packed and ready and—"

"Don't talk like that. We can't."

"You want to go where they're sending you. You want to go."

"For God's sake, how can you talk like that? I don't want to go anyplace, except with you. But we can't run away, Steffy. I've got to face it, whatever it is."

"No you don't. It's noble to be patriotic, sure. It always was. But this is different, Kit. They don't ask for part of your life. Not for two years, or three, or a gamble because maybe you won't ever come back. They ask for all of you, for the rest of your life, forever, and they don't even tell you why. Kit, don't go! We'll hide someplace and get married and—"

"And nothing." Temple stopped the ground-jet, climbed out, opened the door for Stephanie. "Don't you see? There's no place to hide. Wherever you go, they'd look. You wouldn't want to spend the rest of your life running, Steffy. Not with me or anyone else."

"I would. I would!"

"Know what would happen after a few years? We'd hate each other. You'd look at me and say 'I wouldn't be hiding like this, except for you. I'm young and—'"

"Kit, that's cruel! I would not."

"Yes, you would. Steffy, I—" A lump rose in his throat. He'd tell her goodbye, permanently. He had to do it that way, did not want her to wait endlessly and hopelessly for a return that would not materialize. "I didn't get permission to leave, Steffy." He hadn't meant to tell her that, but suddenly it seemed an easy way to break into goodbye.

"What do you mean? No—you didn't . . ."

"I had to see you. What can they do, send me for longer than forever?"

"Then you do want to run away with me!"

"Steffy, no. When I leave you tonight, Steffy, it's for good.

That's it. The last of Kit Temple. Stop thinking about me. I don't exist. I—never was." It sounded ridiculous, even to him.

"Kit, I love you. I love you. How can I forget you?"

"It's happened before. It will happen again." That hurt, too. He was talking about a couple of statistics, not about himself and Stephanie.

"We're different, Kit. I'll love you forever. And—Kit . . . I know you'll come back to me. I'll wait, Kit. We're different. You'll come back."

"How many people do you think said *that* before?"

"You don't want to come back, even if you could. You're not thinking of us at all. You're thinking of your brother."

"You know that isn't true. Sometimes I wonder about Jase, sure. But if I thought there was a chance to return—I'm a selfish cuss, Steffy. If I thought there was a chance, you know I'd want you all for myself. I'd brand you, and that's the truth."

"You do love me!"

"I loved you, Steffy. Kit Temple loved you."

"Loved?"

"Loved. Past tense. When I leave tonight, it's as if I don't exist anymore. As if I never existed. It's got to be that way, Steffy. In thirty years, no one ever returned."

"Including your brother, Jase. So now you want to find him. What do I count for? What . . ."

"This going wasn't my idea. I wanted to stay with you. I wanted to marry you. I can't now. None of it. Forget me, Steffy. Forget you ever knew me. Jase said that to our folks before he was taken." Almost five years before Jason Temple had been selected for the Nowhere Journey. He'd been young, though older than his brother Kit. Young, unattached, almost cheerful he was. Naturally, they never saw him again.

"Hold me, Kit. I'm sorry . . . carrying on like this."

They had walked some distance from the ground-jet,

through scrub oak and bramble bushes. They found a clearing, fragrant-scented, soft-floored still from last autumn, melodic with the chirping of nameless birds. They sat, not talking. Stephanie wore a gay summer dress, full-skirted, cut deep beneath the throat. She swayed toward him from the waist, nestled her head on his shoulder. He could smell the soft, sweet fragrance of her hair, of the skin at the nape of her neck. "If you want to say goodbye . . ." she said.

"Stop it," he told her.

"If you want to say goodbye . . ."

Her head rolled against his chest. She turned, cradled herself in his arms, smiled up at him, squirmed some more and had her head pillowed on his lap. She smiled tremulously, misty-eyed. Her lips parted.

He bent and kissed her, knowing it was all wrong. This was not goodbye, not the way he wanted it. Quickly, definitely, for once and all. With a tear, perhaps, a lot of tears. But permanent goodbye. This was all wrong. The whole idea was to be business-like, objective. It had to be done that way, or no way at all. Briefly, he regretted leaving the encampment.

This wasn't goodbye the way he wanted it. The way it had to be. This was *auf weidersen.*

And then he forgot everything but Stephanie . . .

"I am Alaric Arkalion III," said the extremely young-looking man with the old, wise eyes.

How incongruous, Temple thought. The eyes look almost middle-aged. The rest of him—a boy.

"Something tells me we'll be seeing a lot of each other," Arkalion went on. The voice was that of an older man, too, belying the youthful complexion, the almost childish features, the soft fuzz of a beard.

"I'm Kit Temple," said Temple, extending his hand. "Arkalion, a strange name. I know it from somewhere . . . Say!

Aren't you—don't you have something to do with carpets or something?"

"Here and now, no. I am a number. A-92-6417. But my father is—perhaps I had better say was—my father is Alaric Arkalion II. Yes, that is right, the carpet king."

"I'll be darned," said Temple.

"Why?"

"Well," Temple laughed. "I never met a billionaire before."

"Here I am not a billionaire, nor will I ever be one again. A-92-6417, a number. On his way to Mars with a bunch of other numbers."

"Mars? You sound sure of yourself."

"Reasonably. Ah, it is a pleasure to talk with a gentleman. I am reasonably certain it will be Mars."

Temple nodded in agreement. "That's what the Sunday supplements say, all right."

"And doubtless you have observed no one denies it."

"But what on Earth do we want on Mars?"

"That in itself is a contradiction," laughed Arkalion. "We'll find out, though, Temple."

They had reached the head of the line, found themselves entering a huge, double-decker jet-transport. They found two seats together, followed the instructions printed at the head of the aisle by strapping themselves in and not smoking. Talking all around them was subdued.

"Contrariness has given way to fear," Arkalion observed. "You should have seen them the last few days, waiting around the induction center, a two-ton chip on each shoulder. Say, where *were* you?"

"I—what do you mean?"

"I didn't see you until last evening. Suddenly, you were here."

"Did anyone else miss me?"

"But I remember you the first day."

"Did anyone else miss me? Any of the officials?"

"No. Not that I know of."

"Then I was here," Temple said, very seriously.

Arkalion smiled. "By George, of course. Then you were here. Temple, we'll get along fine."

Temple said that was swell.

"Anyway, we'd better. Forever is a long time."

Three minutes later, the jet took off and soared on eager wings toward the setting sun.

"Men, since we are leaving here in a few hours and since there is no way to get out of the encampment and no place to go over the desert even if you could," the microphone in the great, empty hall boomed as the two files of men marched in, "there is no harm in telling you where you are. From this point, in a limited sense, you shall be kept abreast of your progress.

"We are in White Sands, New Mexico."

"The Garden Spot of the Universe!" someone shouted derisively, remembering the bleak hot desert and jagged mountain peaks as they came down.

"White Sands," muttered Arkalion. "It looks like space travel now, doesn't it, Kit."

Temple shrugged. "Why?"

"White Sands was the center of experiments in rocketry decades ago, when people still talked about those things. Then, for a long time, no one heard anything about White Sands. The rockets grew here, Kit."

"I can readily see why. You could look all your life without finding a barren spot like this."

"Precisely. Someone once called this place—or was it some other place like it?—someone once called it a good place to throw old razor blades. If people still used razor blades."

The microphone blared again, after the several hundred men had entered the great hall and milled about among the echoes. Temple could picture other halls like this, other briefings. "Men, whenever you are given instructions, in here or elsewhere, obey them instantly. Our job is a big one, complicated and exacting. Attention to detail will save us trouble."

Someone said, "My old man served a hitch in the army, back in the sixties. That's what he always said, attention to details. The army is crazy about things like that. Are we in the army or something?"

"This is not the army, but the function is similar," barked the microphone. "Do as you are told and you will get along."

Stirrings in the crowd. Mutterings. Temple gaped. Microphone, yes—but receivers also, placed strategically, all around the hall, to pick up sound. Telio receivers too, perhaps? It made him feel something like a goldfish.

Apparently someone liked the idea of the two-way microphones. "I got a question. When are we coming back?"

Laughter. Hooting. Catcalls.

Blared the microphone: "There is a rotation system in operation, men. When it is feasible, men will be rotated."

"Yeah, in thirty years it ain't been whatsiz—feasible—once!"

"That, unfortunately, is correct. When the situation permits, we will rotate you home."

"From where? Where are we going?"

"At least tell us that."

"Where?"

"How about that?"

There was a pause, then the microphone barked: "I don't know the answer to that question. You won't believe me, but it is the truth. No one knows where you are going. No one. Except the people who are already there."

More catcalls.

"That doesn't make sense," Arkalion whispered. "If it's space travel, the pilots would know, wouldn't they?"

"Automatic?" Temple suggested.

"I doubt it. Space travel must still be new, even if it has thirty years under its belt. If that man speaks the truth— if no one knows . . . just where in the universe *are* we going?"

CHAPTER III

"HEY, looka me. I'm flying!"

"Will you get your big fat feet out of my face?"

"Sure. Show me how to swim away through air, I'll be glad to."

"Leggo that spoon!"

"I ain't got your spoon."

"Will you look at it float away. Hey spoon, hey!"

"Watch this, Charlie. This will get you. I mean, get you."

"What are you gonna do?"

"Relax, chum."

"Leggo my leg. Help! I'm up in the air. Stop that."

"I said relax. There. Ha-ha, lookit him spin, just like a top. All you got to do is get him started and he spins like a top with arms and legs. Top of the morning to you, Charlie. Ha-ha. I said, top of the . . ."

"Someone stop me, I'm getting dizzy."

They floated, tumbled, spun around the spaceship's lounge room in simple, childish glee. They cavorted in festive weightlessness.

"They're happy now," Arkalion observed. "The novelty

of free fall, of weighing exactly nothing, strikes them as amusing."

"I think I'm getting the hang of it," said Temple. Clumsily, he made a few tentative swimming motions in the air, propelling himself forward a few yards before he lost his balance and tumbled head over heels against the wall.

Arkalion came to him quickly, in a combination of swimming and pushing with hands and feet against the wall. Arkalion righted him expertly, sat down gingerly beside him. "If you keep sudden motions to a minimum, you'll get along fine. More than anything else, that's the secret of it."

Temple nodded. "It's sort of like the first time you're on ice skates. Say, how come you're so good at it?"

"I used to read the old, theoretical books on space-travel." The words poured out effortlessly, smoothly. "I'm merely applying the theories put forward as early as the 1950's."

"Oh." But it left Temple with some food for thought. Alaric Arkalion was a queer duck, anyway, and of all the men gathered in the spaceship's lounge, he alone had mastered weightlessness with hardly any trouble.

"Take your ice skates," Arkalion went on. "Some people put them on and use them like natural extensions of their feet the first time. Others fall all over themselves. I suppose I am lucky."

"Sure," said Temple. Actually, the only thing odd about Arkalion was his old-young face and—perhaps—his propensity for coming up with the right answers at the right times. Arkalion had seemed so certain of space-travel. He'd hardly batted an eyelash when they boarded a long, tapering bullet-shaped ship at White Sands and thundered off into the sky. He took for granted the change-over to a huge round ship at the wheel-shaped station in space. Moments after leaving the space station—with a minimum of stress and strain, thanks to the almost-nil gravity—it was Arkalion who first swam through air to the viewport and pointed out the huge cres-

cent earth, green and gray and brown, sparkling with
patches of dazzling silver-white. "You will observe it is a
crescent," Arkalion had said. "It is closer to the sun than
we are, and off at an angle. As I suspected, our destination
is Mars."

Then everyone was saying goodbye to earth. Fantastic,
it seemed. There were tears, there was laughter, cursing,
promises of return, awkward verbal comparisons with the
crescent moon, vows of faithfulness to lovers and sweethearts.
And there was Arkalion, with an avid expression in the old
eyes, Arkalion with his boyish face, not saying goodbye so
much as he was calling hello to something Temple could not
fathom.

Now, as he struggled awkwardly with weightlessness,
Temple called it his imagination. His thought-patterns shifted
vaguely, without motivation, from the gleaming, polished in-
terior of the ship with its smell of antiseptic and metal polish
to the clear Spring air of Earth, blue of sky and bright of
sun. The unique blue sky of Earth which he somehow
knew could not be duplicated elsewhere. Elsewhere—the
word itself bordered on the meaningless.

And Stephanie. The brief warm ecstasy of her—once, forever. He wondered with surprising objectivity if a hundred
other names, a hundred other women were not in a hundred other minds while everyone stared at the crescent
Earth hanging serenely in space—with each name and each
woman as dear as Stephanie, with the same combination of
fire and gentle femininity stirring the blood but saddening
the heart. Would Stephanie really forget him? Did he want
her to? That part of him burned by the fire of her said no
—no, she must not forget him. She was his, his alone, roped
and branded though a universe separated them. But someplace in his heart was the thought, the understanding, the
realization that although Stephanie might keep a small place

for him tucked someplace deep in her emotions, she must
forget. He was gone—permanently. For Stephanie, he was
dead. It was as he had told her that last stolen day. It was
. . . *Stephanie, Stephanie, how much I love you* . . .

Struggling with weightlessness, he made his way back to
the small room he shared with Arkalion. Hardly more than
a cubicle, it was, with sufficient room for two beds, a sink,
a small chest. He lay down and slept, murmuring Stephanie's
name in his sleep.

He awoke to the faint hum of the air-pumps, got up feeling
rested, forgot his weightlessness and floated to the ceiling
where only an outthrust arm prevented a nasty bump on his
head. He used hand grips on the wall to let himself down. He
washed, aware of no way to prevent the water he splashed
on his face from forming fine droplets and spraying the entire room. When he crossed back to the foot of his bed to
get his towel he thrust one foot out too rapidly, lost his balance, half-rose, stumbled and fell against the other bed
which, like all other items of furniture, was fastened to the
floor. But his elbow struck sleeping Arkalion's jaw sharply,
hard enough to jar the man's teeth.

"I'm sorry," said Temple. "Didn't mean to do that," he
apologized again, feeling embarrassed.

Arkalion merely lay there.

"I said I'm sorry."

Arkalion still slept. It seemed inconceivable, for Temple's
elbow pained him considerably. He bent down, examined
his inert companion.

Arkalion stirred not a muscle.

Vaguely alarmed, Temple thrust a hand to Arkalion's chest,
felt nothing. He crouched, rested the side of his head over
Arkalion's heart. He listened, heard—nothing.

What was going on here?

"Hey, Arkalion!" Temple shook him, gently at first, then

with savage force. Weightless, Arkalion's body floated up off the bed, taking the covers with it. His own heart pounding furiously, Temple got it down again, fingered the left wrist and swallowed nervously.

Temple had never seen a dead man before. Arkalion's heart did not beat. Arkalion had no pulse.

Arkalion was dead.

Yelling hoarsely, Temple plunged from the room, soaring off the floor in his haste and striking his head against the ceiling hard enough to make him see stars. "This guy is dead!" he cried. "Arkalion is dead."

Men stirred in the companionway. Someone called for one of the armed guards who were constantly on patrol.

"If he's dead, you're yelling loud enough to get him out of his grave." The voice was quiet, amused.

Arkalion.

"What?" Temple blurted, whirling around and striking his head again. A little wild-eyed, he re-entered the room.

"Now, who is dead, Kit?" demanded Arkalion, sitting up and stretching comfortably.

"Who—is dead? Who—?" Open-mouthed, Temple stared.

A guard, completely at home with weightlessness, entered the cubicle briskly. "What's the trouble in here? Something about a dead man, they said."

"A dead man?" demanded Arkalion. "Indeed."

"Dead?" muttered Temple, lamely and foolishly. "Dead . . ."

Arkalion smiled deprecatingly. "My friend must have been talking in his sleep. The only thing dead in here is my appetite. Weightlessness doesn't let you become very hungry."

"You'll grow used to it," the guard promised. He patted his paunch happily. "I am. Well, don't raise the alarm unless there's some trouble. Remember about the boy who cried wolf."

"Of course," said Temple. "Sure. Sorry."

He watched the guard depart.

"Bad dream?" Arkalion wanted to know.

"Bad dream, my foot. I accidentally hit you. Hard enough to hurt. You didn't move."

"I'm a sound sleeper."

"I felt for your heart. It wasn't beating. It wasn't!"

"Oh, come, come."

"Your heart was not beating, I said."

"And I suppose I was cold as a slab of ice?"

"Umm, no. I don't remember. Maybe you were. You had no pulse, either."

Arkalion laughed easily. "And am I still dead?"

"Well—"

"Clearly a case of overwrought nerves and a highly keyed imagination. What you need is some more sleep."

"I'm not sleepy, thanks."

"Well, I think I'll get up and go down for breakfast." Arkalion climbed out of bed gingerly, made his way to the sink and was soon gargling with a bottle of prepared mouthwash, occasionally spraying weightless droplets of the pink liquid up at the ceiling.

Temple lit a cigarette with shaking fingers, made his way to Arkalion's bed while the man hummed tunelessly at the sink. Temple let his hands fall on the sheet. It was not cold, but comfortably cool. Hardly as warm as it should have been, with a man sleeping on it all night.

Was he still imagining things?

"I'm glad you didn't call for a burial detail and have me expelled into space with yesterday's garbage," Arkalion called over his shoulder jauntily as he went outside for some breakfast.

Temple cursed softly and lit another cigarette, dropping the first one into a disposal chute on the wall.

Every night thereafter, Temple made it a point to remain awake after Arkalion apparently had fallen asleep. But if he were seeking repetition of the peculiar occurrence, he was disappointed. Not only did Arkalion sleep soundly and through the night, but he snored. Loudly and clearly, a wheezing snore.

Arkalion's strange feat—or his own overwrought imagination, Temple thought wryly—was good for one thing: it took his mind off Stephanie. The days wore on in endless, monotonous routine. He took some books from the ship's library and browsed through them, even managing to find one concerned with traumatic catalepsy, which stated that a severe emotional shock might render one into a deep enough trance to have a layman mistakenly pronounce him dead. But what had been the severe emotional disturbance for Arkalion? Could the effects of weightlessness manifest themselves in that way in rare instances? Temple naturally did not know, but he resolved to find out if he could after reaching their destination.

One day—it was three weeks after they left the space station, Temple realized—they were all called to assembly in the ship's large main lounge. As the men drifted in, Temple was amazed to see the progress they had made with weightlessness. He himself had advanced to handy facility in locomotion, but it struck him all the more pointedly when he saw two hundred men swim and float through air, pushing themselves along by means of the hand-holds strategically placed along the walls.

The ever-present microphone greeted them all. "Good afternoon, men."

"Good afternoon, mac!"

"Hey, is this the way to Ebbetts' Field?"

"Get on with it!"

"Sounds like the same man who addressed us in White Sands," Temple told Arkalion. "He sure does get around."

"A recording, probably. Listen."

"Our destination, as you've probably read in newspapers and magazines, is the planet Mars."

Mutterings in the assembly, not many of surprise.

"Their suppositions, based both on the seven hundred eighty day lapse between Nowhere Journeys and the romantic position in which the planet Mars has always been held, are correct. We are going to Mars.

"For most of you, Mars will be a permanent home for many years to come—"

"Most of us?" Temple wondered out loud.

Arkalion raised a finger to his lips for silence.

"—until such time as you are rotated according to the policy of rotation set up by the government."

Temple had grown accustomed to the familiar hoots and catcalls. He almost had an urge to join in himself.

"Interesting," Arkalion pointed out. "Back at White Sands they claimed not to know our destination. They knew it all right—up to a point. The planet Mars. But now they say that all of us will not remain on Mars. Most interesting."

"—further indoctrination in our mission soon after our arrival on the red planet. Landing will be performed under somewhat less strain than the initial takeoff in the Earth-to-station ferry, since Mars exerts less of a gravity pull than Earth. On the other hand, you have been weightless for three weeks and the change-over is liable to make some of you sick. It will pass harmlessly enough.

"We realize it is difficult, being taken from your homes without knowing the nature of your urgent mission. All I can tell you now—and, as a matter of fact, all I know—"

"Here we go again," said Temple. "More riddles."

"—is that everything *is* of the utmost urgency. Our entire way of life is at stake. Our job will be to safeguard it. In the months which follow, few of you will have any big, significant role to play, but all of you, working together, will provide the strength we need. When the *cadre—*"

"So they call their guards teachers," Arkalion commented dryly.

"—come around, they will see that each man is strapped properly into his bunk for deceleration. Deceleration begins in twenty-seven minutes."

Mars, thought Temple, back in his room with Arkalion. *Mars*. He did not think of Stephanie, except as a man who knows he must spend the rest of his life in prison might think of a lush green field, or the cool swish of skis over fresh, powdery snow, or the sound of yardarms creaking against the wind on a small sailing schooner, or the tang of wieners roasting over an open fire with the crisp air of fall against your back, or the scent of good French brandy, or a woman.

Deceleration began promptly. Before his face was distorted and his eyes forced shut by a pressure of four gravities, Temple had time to see the look of complete unconcern on Arkalion's face. Arkalion, in fact, was sleeping.

He seemed as completely relaxed as he did that morning Temple thought he was dead.

CHAPTER IV

"PETROVITCH, S. A.!" called the Comrade standing abreast of the head of the line, a thin, nervous man half a head shorter than the girl herself. Sophia Androvna Petrovitch strode forward, took a pair of trim white shorts from the neat stack at his left.

"Is that all?" she said, looking at him.

"Yes, Comrade. Well, a woman. Well."

Without embarrassment, Sophia had seen the men ahead of her in line strip and climb into the white shorts before they disappeared through a portal ahead of the line, depositing their clothing in a growing pile on the floor. But now it was Sophia's turn, after almost a two hour wait. Not that it was chilly, but . . .

"Is that all?" she repeated.

"Certainly. Strip and move along, Comrade." The nervous little man appraised her lecherously, she thought.

"Then I must keep some of my own clothing," she told him.

"Impossible. I have my orders."

"I am a woman."

"You are a volunteer for the Stalintrek. You will take no personal property—no clothing—with you. Strip and advance, please."

Sophia flushed slightly, while the men behind her began to call and taunt.

"I like this Stalintrek."

"Oh, yes."

"We are waiting, Comrade."

Quickly and with an objective detachment which surprised her, Sophia unbuttoned her shirt, removed it. Her one wish —and an odd one, she thought, smiling—was for wax for her ears. She loosened the three snaps of her skirt, watched it fall to the floor. She stood there briefly, lithe-limbed, a tall, slim girl, then had the white shorts over her nakedness in one quick motion. She still wore a coarse halter.

"All personal effects, Comrade," said the nervous little man.

"No," Sophia told him.

"But yes. Definitely, yes. You hold up the line, and we have a schedule to maintain. The Stalintrek demands quick, prompt obedience."

"Then you will give me one additional item of clothing."

The man looked at Sophia's halter, at the fine way she filled it. He shrugged. "We don't have it," he said, clearly enjoying himself.

In volunteering for the Stalintrek, Sophia had invaded man's domain. She had watched not with embarrassment but with scorn while the men in front of her got out of their clothing. She had invaded man's domain, and as she watched them, the short flabby ones, the bony ones with protruding ribs and collar-bones, those of milky white skin and soft hands, she knew most of them would bite off more than they could chew if ever they tried what was the most natural thing for men to try with a lone woman in an isolated environment. But she *was* in a man's world now, and if that was the way they wanted it, she would ask no quarter.

She reached up quickly with one hand and unfastened the halter, catching it with her free hand and holding it in front of her breasts while the nervous little man licked his lips and gaped. Sophia grabbed another pair of the white shorts, tore it quickly with her strong fingers, fashioning a crude covering for herself. This she pulled around her, fastening it securely with a knot in back.

"You'll have to give that back to me," declared the nervous little Comrade.

"I'll bet you a samovar on that," Sophia said quietly, so only the man heard her.

He reached out, as if to rip the crude halter from her body, but Sophia met him halfway with her strong, slim fingers, wrapping them around his biceps and squeezing. The man's face turned quickly to white as he tried unsuccessfully to free his arm.

"Please, that hurts."

"I keep what I am wearing." She tightened her grip, but gazed serenely into space as the man stifled a whimper.

"Well—" the man whispered indecisively as he gritted his teeth.

"Fool!" said Sophia. "Your arm will be black and blue for a week. While you men grow soft and lazy, many of the women take their gymnastics seriously, especially if they want to keep their figures with the work they must do and the food they must eat. I am stronger than you and I will hurt you unless—" And her hand tightened around his scrawny arm until her knuckles showed white.

"Wear what you have and go," the man pleaded, and moaned softly when Sophia released his numb arm and strode through the portal, still drawing whistles and leers from the other men, who missed the by-play completely.

"So we're on Mars!"

"It ain't Nowhere after all, it's Mars."

"Wait and see, buster. Wait and see."

"Kind of cold, isn't it? Well, if this was Venus and some of them beautiful one-armed dames was waiting for us—"

"That's just a statue, stupid."

"Lookit all them people down there, will you?"

"You think they're Martians?"

"Stupid! We ain't the first ones went on the Nowhere Journey."

"What are we waiting for? It sure will feel good to stretch your legs."

"Let's go!"

"Look out, Mars, here I come!"

It would have been just right for a Hollywood epic, Temple thought. The rusty ochre emptiness spreading out toward the horizon in all directions, spotted occasionally with pale green and frosty white, the sky gray with but a shade of blue in it, distant gusts of Martian wind swirling ochre clouds across the desert, the spaceship poised on its ungainly bottom, a great silver bowling ball with rocket tubes for finger holes, and the Martians from Earth who had been here on this alien world for seven-hundred-eighty days or twice seven-eighty or three times, and who fought in frenzied eagerness, like savages, to reach the descending gangplank first.

Earth chorus: Hey, Martians, any of you guys speak English? Hah-ha, I said, any of you guys . . .

Where are all them canals I heard so much about?

You think maybe they're dangerous? (Laughter)

No dames. Hey, no dames . . .

Who were you expecting, Donna Daunley?

What kind of place is Mars with no women?"

What do they do here, anyway, just sit around and wait for the next rocket?

I'm cold.

Get used to it, brother, get used to it.

Look out, Mars, here I come!

Martian chorus: Who won the Series last year, Detroit?

Hey, bud, tell me, are dames still wearing those one piece things, all colors, so you see their legs up to about here and their chests down to about here? (Gestures lewdly)

Which one of you guys can tell me what it's like to take a bath? I mean a real bath in a real bath tub.

Hey, we licked Russia yet?

We heard they were gonna send some dames!

Dames—ha-ha, you're breaking my heart.

Tell me what a steak tastes like. So thick.

Me? Gimme a bowl of steamed oysters. And a dame.

Dames. Girls. Women. Females. Chicks. Tomatoes. Frails. Dames. Dames. Dames . . .

They did not seem to mind the cold, these Earth-Martians. Temple guessed they never spent much time out of doors (above ground, for there were no buildings?) because all seemed pale and white. While the sun was weaker, so was the protection offered by a thinner atmosphere. The sun's actinic rays could burn, and so could the sand-driving wind. But pale skins could not be the result of staying indoors, for Temple noted the lack of man-made structures at once. Underground, then. The Earth-Martians lived underground like moles. Doing what? And for what reason? With what ultimate goal, if any? And where did those men who did not remain on Mars go? Temple's head whirled with countless questions—and no answers.

Shoulder to shoulder with Arkalion, he made his way down the gangplank, turning up the collar of his jumper against the stinging wind.

"You got any newspapers, pal?"

"Magazines?"

"Phonograph records?"

"Gossip?"

"Newsfilm?"

"Who's the heavyweight champ?"

"We lick those Commies in Burma yet?"

"Step back! Watch that man. Maybe he's your replacement."

"Replacement. Ha-ha. That's good."

All types of men. All ages. In torn, tattered clothing, mostly. In rags. Even if a man seemed more well-groomed than the rest, on closer examination Temple could see the careful stitching, the patches, the fades and stains. No one seemed to mind.

"Hey, bud. What do you hear about rotation? They passed any laws yet?"

"I been here ten years. When do I get rotated?"

"Ain't that something? Dad Jenks came here with the first ship. Don't you talk about rotation. Ask Dad."

"Better not mention that word to Dad Jenks. He sees red."

"This whole damn planet is red."

"Want a guided tour of nowhere, men? Step right up."

Arkalion grinned. "They seem so well-adjusted," he said, then shuddered against the cold and followed Temple, with the others, through the crowd.

They were inoculated against nameless diseases. (Watch for the needle with the hook)

They were told again they had arrived on the planet Mars. (No kidding?)

Led to a drab underground city, dimly lit, dank, noisome with mold and mildew. (Quick, the chlorophyll)

Assigned bunks in a dormitory, with four men to a room. (Be it ever so humble—bah!)

Told to keep things clean and assigned temporarily to a garbage pickup detail. (For this I left Sheboygan?)

Read to from the Declaration of Independence, the Constitution and Public Law 1182 (concerned with the Nowhere Journey, it told them nothing they did not already know).

Given as complete a battery of tests, mental, emotional and physical, as Temple ever knew existed. (Cripes, man! How the hell should I know what the cube root of—5 is? I never finished high school!)

Subjected to an exhaustive, overlong, and at times meaningless personal interview. (No doc, honest. I never knew I had a—uh—anxiety neurosis. Is it dangerous?)

"How do you do, Temple? Sit down."

"Thank you."

"Thought you'd like to know that while your overall test score is not uncanny, it's decidedly high."

"So what?"

"So nothing—not necessarily. Except that with it you have a very well balanced personality. We can use you, Temple."

"That's why I'm here."

"I mean—elsewhere. Mars is only a way station, a training center for a select few. It takes an awful lot of administrative work to keep this place going, which explains the need for all the station personnel."

"Listen. The last few weeks I had everything thrown at me. Everything, the works. Mind answering one question?"

"Shoot."

"What's this all about?"

"Temple, I don't know!"

"You what?"

"I know you find it hard to believe, but I don't. There isn't a man here on Mars who knows the whole story, either—and certainly not on Earth. We know enough to keep everything in operation. And we know it's important, all of it, everything we do."

"You mentioned a need for some men elsewhere. Where?"

The psychiatrist shrugged. "I don't know. Somewhere. Anywhere." He spread his hands out eloquently. "That's where the Nowhere Journey comes in."

"Surely you can tell me something more than—"

"Absolutely not. It isn't that I don't want to. I can't. I don't know."

"Well, one more question I'd like you to answer."

The psychiatrist lit a cigarette, grinned. "Say, who is interviewing whom?"

"This one I think you can tackle. I have a brother, Jason Temple. Embarked on the Nowhere Journey five years ago. I wonder—"

"So that's the one factor in your psychograph we couldn't figure out—anxiety over your brother."

"I doubt it," shrugged Temple. "More likely my fiancee."

"Umm, common enough. You were to be married?"

"Yes." *Stephanie, what are you doing now? Right now?*

"That's what hurts the most . . . Well, yes, I can find out about your brother." The psychiatrist flicked a toggle on his desk. "Jamison, find what you can on Temple, Jason, year of—"

"1987," Temple supplied.

"1987. We'll wait."

After a moment or two, the voice came through, faintly metallic: "Temple, Jason. Arrival: 1987. Psychograph, 115-b12. Mental aggregate, 98. Physcom, good to excellent. Training: two years, space perception concentrate, others. Shipped out: 1989."

So Jase had shipped out for—Nowhere.

"Someday you'll follow in your brother's footsteps, Temple. Now, though, I have a few hundred questions I'd like you to answer."

The psychiatrist hadn't exaggerated. Several hours of questioning followed. Once reminded of her, Temple found it hard to keep his thought off Stephanie.

He left the psychiatrist's office more confused than ever.

"Good morning, child. You are Stephanie Andrews?" Stepphanie hadn't felt up to working that first morning after Kit's final goodbye. She answered the door in her bathrobe, saw a small, middle-aged woman with graying hair and a kind face. "That's right. Won't you come in?"

"Thank you. I represent the Complete Emancipation League, Miss Andrews."

"Complete Emancipation League? Oh, something to do with politics. Really, I'm not much interested in—"

"That's entirely the trouble," declared the older woman. "Too many of us are not interested in politics. I'd like to discuss the C.E.L. with you, my dear, if you will bear with me a few minutes."

"All right," said Stephanie. "Would you like a glass of sherry?"

"In the morning?" the older woman smiled.

"I'm sorry. Don't mind me. My fiance left yesterday, took his final goodbye. He—he embarked on the Nowhere Journey."

"I realize that. It is precisely why I am here. My dear, the C.E.L. does not want to fight the government. If the government decides that the Nowhere Journey is vital for the welfare of the country—even if the government won't or can't explain what the Nowhere Journey is—that's all right with us. But if the government says there is a rotation system but does absolutely nothing about it, we're interested in that. Do you follow me?"

"Yes!" cried Stephanie. "Oh, yes. Go on."

"The C.E.L. has sixty-eight people in Congress for the current term. We hope to raise that number to seventy-five for next election. It's a long fight, a slow uphill fight, and frankly, my dear, we need all the help we can get. People —young women like yourself, my dear—are entirely too lethargic, if you'll forgive me."

"You ought to forgive *me*," said Stephanie, "if you will. You know, it's funny. I had vague ideas about helping Kit, about finding some way to get him back. Only to tackle something like that alone . . . I'm only twenty-one, just a girl, and I don't know anyone important. No one ever comes back, that's what you hear. But there's a rotation system, you also hear that. If I can be of any help . . ."

"You certainly can, my dear. We'd be delighted to have you."

"Then, eventually, maybe, just maybe, we'll start getting them rotated home?"

"We can't promise a thing. We can only try. And I never did say we'd try to get the boys rotated, my dear. There is a rotation system in the law, right there in Public Law 1182. But if no men have ever been rotated, there must be a reason for it."

"Yes, but—"

"But we'll see. If for some reason rotation simply is not practicable, we'll find another way. Which is why we call ourselves the C.E.L.—Complete Emancipation League—for women. If men must embark on the Nowhere Journey—the least they can do is let their women volunteer to go along with them if they want to—since it may be forever. Let a bunch of women get to this Nowhere place and you'll never know what might happen, that's what I say."

Something about the gray haired woman's earthly confidence imbued Stephanie with an optimism she never expected. "Well," she said, smiling, "if we can't bring ourselves to Mohammed . . . No, that's all wrong! . . . to the mountain . . . ?"

"Yes, there's an old saying. But it isn't important. You get the idea. My dear, how would you like to go to Nowhere?"

"I—to Kit, anywhere, anywhere!" *I'll never forget yesterday, Kit darling. Never!*

"I make no promises, Stephanie, but it may be sooner than you think. Morning be hanged, perhaps I will have some sherry after all. Umm, you wouldn't by any chance have some Canadian instead?"

Humming, Stephanie dashed into the kitchen for some glasses.

There were times when the real Alaric Arkalion III wished his father would mind his own business. Like that thing about the Nowhere Journey, for instance. Maybe Alaric Sr. didn't realize it, but being the spoiled son of a billionaire wasn't all fun. "I'm a dilettante," Alaric would tell himself often, gazing in the mirror, "a bored dilettante at the age of twenty-one."

Which in itself, he had to admit, wasn't too bad. But having reneged on the Nowhere Journey in favor of a stranger twice his age who now carried his, Alaric's face, had engendered some annoying complications. "You'll either have to hide or change your own appearance and identity, Alaric."

"Hide? For how long, father?"

"I can't be sure. Years, probably."

"That's crazy. I'm not going to hide for years."

"Then change your appearance. Your way of life. Your occupation."

"I have no occupation."

"Get one. Change your face, too. Your fingerprints. It can be done. Become a new man, live a new life."

In hiding there was boredom, impossible boredom. In the other alternative there was adventure, intrigue—but uncertainty. One part of young Alaric craved that uncertainty, the rest of him shunned it. In a way it was like the Nowhere Journey all over again.

"Maybe Nowhere wouldn't have been so bad," said Alaric to his father, choosing as a temporary alternative and retreat what he knew couldn't possibly happen.

Couldn't it?

"If I choose another identity, I'd be eligible again for the Nowhere Journey."

"By George, I hadn't considered that. No, wait. You could be older than twenty-six."

"I like it the way I am," Alaric said, pouting.

"Then you'll have to hide. I spent ten million dollars to secure your future, Alaric. I don't want you to throw it away."

Alaric pouted some more. "Let me think about it."

"Fair enough, but I'll want your answer tomorrow. Meanwhile, you are not to leave the house."

Alaric agreed verbally, but took the first opportunity which presented itself—that very night—to sneak out the servants' door, go downtown, and get stewed to the gills.

At two in the morning he was picked up by the police for disorderly conduct (it had happened before) after losing a fistfight to a much poorer, much meaner drunk in a downtown bar. They questioned Alaric at the police station, examined his belongings, went through his wallet, notified his home.

Fuming, Alaric Sr. rushed to the police station to get his

son. He was met by the desk sergeant, a fat, balding man who wore his uniform in a slovenly fashion.

"Mr. Arkalion?" demanded the sergeant, picking at his teeth with a toothpick.

"Yes. I have come for Alaric, my son."

"Sure. Sure. But your son's in trouble, Mr. Arkalion. Serious trouble."

"What are you talking about? If there are any damages, I'll pay. He didn't—hurt, anyone, did he?"

The sergeant broke the toothpick between his teeth, laughed. "Him? Naw. He got the hell beat out of him by a drunk half his size. It ain't that kind of trouble, Mr. Arkalion. You know what an 1182 card is, mister?"

Arkalion's face drained white. "Why—yes."

"Alaric's got one."

"Naturally."

"According to the card, he should have shipped out on the Nowhere Journey, mister. He didn't. He's in serious trouble."

"I'll see the district attorney."

"More'n likely, you'll see the attorney general. Serious trouble."

CHAPTER V

THE TROUBLE with the Stalintrek, Sophia thought, was that it took months to get absolutely nowhere. There had been the painful pressure, the loss of consciousness, the confinement in this tight little world of domitories and gleaming metal walls, the uncanny feeling of no weight, the ability —boring after a while, but interesting at first—to float about in air almost at will.

Then, how many months of sameness? Sophia had lost all track of time through *ennui*. But for the first brief period of adjustment on the part of her fellows to the fact that although she was a woman and shared their man's life she was still to be inviolate, the routine had been anything but exciting. The period of adjustment had had its adventures, its uncertainties, its challenge, and to Sophia it had been stimulating. Why was it, she wondered, that the men who carried their sex with strength and dignity, the hard-muscled men who could have their way with her if they resorted to force were the men who did not violate her privacy, while the weaklings, the softer, smaller men, or the average men whom Sophia considered her physical equals were the ones who gave her trouble?

She had always accepted her beauty, the obvious attraction men found in her, with an objective unconcern. She had been endowed with sex appeal; there was not much room in her life to exploit it, even had she wanted to. Now, now when she wanted anything but that, it gave her trouble.

Her room was shared, of necessity, with three men. Tall, gangling Boris gave her no trouble, turned his back when she undressed for the evening, even though she was careful to slip under the covers first. Ivan, the second man, was short, thin, stooped. Often she found him looking at her with what might have been more than a healthy interest, but aside from that he kept his peace. Besides, Ivan had spent two years in secondary school (as much as Sophia) and she enjoyed conversing with him.

The third man, Georgi, was the troublemaker. Georgi was one of those plump young men with red cheeks, big, eager eyes, a voice somewhat too high. He was an avid talker, a boaster and a boor. In the beginning he showered attentions on Sophia. He insisted on drawing her wash-basin at night, escorted her to breakfast every morning, told her in confidence of the conquests he had made over beautiful women (but not as beautiful as you, Sophia). He soon began to take liberties. He would sit—timorously at first, but with growing boldness—on the corner of her bed, talking with her at night after the others had retired, Ivan with his snores, Boris with his strong, deep breathing. And night after night, plump Georgi grew bolder.

He would reach out and touch Sophia, he would insist on tucking her in at night (let me be your big brother), he would awaken her in the morning with his hand heavy on her shoulder. Finally, one night at bedtime, she heard him conversing in low whispers with Ivan and Boris. She could not hear the words, but Boris looked at her with what she thought was surprise, Ivan nodded in an understanding way, and both of them left the room.

Sophia frowned. "What did you tell them, Georgi?"

"That we wanted to be alone one evening, of course."

"I never gave you any indication—"

"I could see it in your eyes, in the way you looked at me."

"Well, you had better call them back inside and go to bed."

Georgi shook his head, approached her.

"Georgi! Call them back or I will."

"No, you won't." Georgi followed her as she retreated into a corner of the room. When she reached the wall and could retreat no further, he placed his thick hands on her shoulders, drew her to him slowly. "You will call no one," he rasped.

She ducked under his arms, eluded him, was on the point of running to the door, throwing it open and shouting, when she considered. If she did, she would be asking for quarter, gaining a temporary reprieve, inviting the same sort of thing all over again.

She crossed to the bed and sat down. "Come here, Georgi."

"Ah." He came to her.

She watched him warily, a soft flabby man not quite so tall as she was, but who nevertheless outweighed her by thirty or forty pounds. In his eagerness, he walked too fast, lost his footing and floated gently to the ceiling. Smiling as demurely as she could, Sophia reached up, circled his ankle with her hand.

"I never could get used to this weightlessness," Georgi admitted. "Be nice and pull me down."

"I will be nice. I will teach you a lesson."

He weighed exactly nothing. It was as simple as stretching. Sophia merely extended her arm upwards and Georgi's head hit the ceiling with a loud *thunk*. Georgi groaned. Sophia repeated the procedure, lowering her arm a foot—and Georgi with it—then raising it and bouncing his head off the ceiling.

"I don't understand," Georgi whined, trying to break free but only succeeding in thrashing his chubby arms foolishly.

"You haven't mastered weightlessness," Sophia smiled up at him. "I have. I said I would teach you a lesson. First make sure you have the strength of a man if you would play a man's game."

Still smiling, Sophia commenced spinning the hand which held Georgi's ankle. Arms and free leg flailing air helplessly, Georgi began to spin.

"Put me down!" he whined, a boy now, not even pretending to be a man. When Sophia shoved out gently and let his ankle go he did a neat flip in air and hung suspended, upside down, his feet near the ceiling, his head on a level with Sophia's shoulders. He cried.

She slapped his upside down face, carefully and without excitement, reddening the cheeks. "I was—only joking," he slobbered. "Call back our friends."

Sophia found one of the hard, air-tight metal flasks they used for drinking in weightlessness. With one hand she opened the lid, with the other she grasped Georgi's shoulder and spun him in air, still upside down. She squirted the water in his face, and because he was upside down and yelling it made him choke and cough. When the container was empty she lowered Georgi gently to the floor.

Minutes later, she opened the door, summoned Boris and Ivan, who came into the room self-consciously. What they found was a thoroughly beaten Georgi sobbing on the floor. After that, Sophia had no trouble. Week after week of boredom followed and she almost wished Georgi or someone else would *look* for trouble . . . even if it were something she could not handle, for although she was stronger than average and more beautiful, she was still a woman first, and she knew if the right man . . .

"Did you know that radio communication is maintained between Earth and Mars?" the Alaric Arkalion on Mars asked Temple.

"Why, no. I never thought about it."

"It is, and I am in some difficulty."

"What's the matter?" Temple had grown to like Arkalion, despite the man's peculiarities. He had given up trying to figure him out, feeling that the only way he'd get anywhere was with Arkalion's cooperation.

"It's a long story which I'm afraid you would not altogether understand. The authorities on Earth don't think I belong here on the Nowhere Journey."

"Is that so? A mistake, huh? I sure am glad for you, Alaric."

"That's not the difficulty. It seems that there is the matter of impersonation, of violating some of the clauses in Public Law 1182. You're glad for me. I'm likely to go to prison."

"If it's that serious, how come they told you?"

"They didn't. But I—managed to find out. I won't go into

details, Kit, but obviously, if I managed to embark for Nowhere when I didn't have to, then I wanted to go. Right?"

"I—uh, guess so. But why—?"

"That isn't the point. I *still* want to go. Not to Mars, but to Nowhere. I still can, despite what has happened, but I need help."

Temple said, "Anything I can do, I'll be glad to," and meant it. For one thing, he liked Arkalion. For another, Arkalion seemed to know more, much more than he would ever say—unless Temple could win his confidence. For a third, Temple was growing sick and tired of Mars with its drab ochre sameness (when he got to the surface, which was rarely), with its dank underground city, with its meaningless attention to meaningless detail. Either way, he figured there was no returning to Earth. If Nowhere meant adventure, as he suspected it might, it would be preferable. Mars might have been the other end of the galaxy for all its nearness to Earth, anyway.

"There is a great deal you can do. But you'll have to come with me."

"Where?" Temple demanded.

"Where you will go eventually. To Nowhere."

"Fine." And Temple smiled. "Why not now as well as later?"

"I'll be frank with you. If you go now, you go untrained. You may need your training. Undoubtedly, you will."

"You know a lot more than you want to talk about, don't you?"

"Frankly, yes . . . I am sorry, Kit."

"That's all right. You have your reasons. I guess if I go with you I'll find out soon enough, anyway."

Arkalion grinned. "You have guessed correctly. I am going to Nowhere, before they return me to Earth for prosecution under Public Law 1182. I cannot go alone, for it takes at least two to operate . . . well, you'll see."

"Count me in," said Temple.

"Remember, you may one day wish you had remained on Mars for your training."

"I'll take my chances. Mars is driving me crazy. All I do is think of Earth and Stephanie."

"Then come."

"Where are we going?"

"A long, long way off. It is unthinkably remote, this place called Nowhere."

Temple felt suddenly like a kid playing hookey from school. "Lead on," he said, almost jauntily. He knew he was leaving Stephanie still further behind, but had he been in prison on the next street to hers, he might as well have been a million miles away.

As for Arkalion—the thought suddenly struck Temple—Arkalion wasn't necessarily leaving his world further behind. Perhaps Arkalion was going home . . .

Stephanie picked up the phone eagerly. In the weeks since her first meeting with Mrs. Draper of the C.E.L., the older woman had been a fountain of information and of hope for her. Stephanie for her part had taken over Mrs. Draper's job in her own section of Center City: she was busy contacting the two hundred mothers and fifty sweethearts of the Nowhere Journey which had taken Kit from her. And now Mrs. Draper had called with information.

"We've successfully combined forces with some of the less militant elements in both houses of Congress," Mrs. Draper told her over the phone. "Do you realize, my dear, this marks the first time the C.E.L. has managed to put something constructive through Congress? Until now we've been content merely to block legislation, such as an increase in the Nowhere contingent from . . ."

"Yes, Mrs. Draper. I know all that. But what about this constructive thing you've done."

"Well, my dear, don't count your chickens. But we *have* passed the bill, and we expect the President won't veto it. You see, the President has two nephews who . . ."

"I know. I know. What bill did you pass?"

"Unfortunately, it's somewhat vague. Ultimately, the Nowhere Commission must do the deciding, but it does pave the way."

"For what, Mrs. Draper?"

"Hold onto your hat, my dear. The bill authorizes the Nowhere Commission to make as much of a study as it can of conditions—wherever our boys are sent."

"Oh." Stephanie was disappointed. "That won't get them back to us."

"No. You're right, it won't get them back to us. That isn't the idea at all, for there is more than one way to skin a cat, my dear. The Nowhere Commission will be studying conditions—"

"How can they? I thought everything was so hush-hush, not even Congress knew anything about it."

"That was the first big hurdle we have apparently overcome. Anyway, they will be studying conditions with a view of determining if one girl—just one, mind you—can embark on the Nowhere Journey as a pilot study and—"

"But I thought they could make the journey only once every seven-hundred-eighty days."

"Get Congress aroused and you can move mountains. It seems the expense entailed in a trip at any but those times is generally prohibitive, but when something special comes up—"

"It can be done! Mrs. Draper, how I love to talk with you!"

"See? There you go, my dear, counting your chickens. One girl will be sent, if the study indicates she can take it. *One* girl, Stephanie, and only after a study. She'd merely be a pilot case. But afterwards . . . Ah, afterwards . . .

Perhaps someday soon qualified women will be able to join their men in Nowhere."

"Mrs. Draper, I love you."

"Naturally, you will tell all this to prospective C.E.L. members. Now we have something concrete to work with."

"I know. And I will, I will, Mrs. Draper. By the way, how are they going to pick the girl, the one girl?"

"Don't count your chickens, for Heaven's sake! They haven't even studied the situation yet. Well, I'll call you, my dear."

Stephanie hung up, dressed, went about her canvassing. She thought happy thoughts all week.

"Shh! Quiet," cautioned Arkalion, leading the way down a flight of heavy-duty plastic stairs.

"How do you know your way around here so well?"

"I said quiet."

It was not so much, Temple realized, that Arkalion was really afraid of making noise. Rather, he did not want to answer questions.

Temple smiled in the semi-darkness, heard the steady drip-drip-drip of water off somewhere to his left. Eons before the coming of man on this stopover point to Nowhere, the Martian waters had retreated from the planet's ancient surface and seeped underground to carve, slow drop by drop, the caverns which honey-combed the planet. "You know your way around so well, I'd swear you were a Martian."

Arkalion's soft laugh carried far. "I said there was to be no noise. Please! As for the Martians, the only Martians are here all around you, the men of Earth. Ahh, here we are."

At the bottom of the flight of stairs Temple could see a door, metallic, giving the impression of strength without great weight. Arkalion paused a moment, did something with a series of levers, shook his head impatiently, started all over again.

"What's that for?" Temple wanted to know.

"What do you think? It is a combination lock, with five million possible combinations. Do you want to be here for all of eternity?"

"No."

"Then quiet."

Vaguely, Temple wondered why the door wasn't guarded.

"With a lock like this," Arkalion explained, as if he had read Temple's thought, "they need no other precaution. It is assumed that only authorized personnel know the combination."

Then had Arkalion come this way before? It seemed the only possible assumption. But when? And how? "Here we are," said Arkalion.

The door swung in toward them.

Temple strode forward, found himself in a great bare hall, surprisingly well-lighted. After the dimness of the caverns, he hardly could see.

"Don't stand there scowling and fussing with your eyes. There is one additional precaution—an alarm at Central Headquarters. We have about five minutes, no more."

At one end of the bare hall stood what to Temple looked for all the world like an old-fashioned telephone booth, except that its walls were completely opaque. On the wall adjacent to it was a single lever with two positions marked "hold" and "transport". The lever stood firmly in the "hold" position.

"You sure you want to come?" Arkalion demanded.

"Yes, I told you that."

"Good. I have no time to explain. I will enter the conveyor."

"Conveyor?"

"This booth. You will wait until the door is shut, then

pull the lever down. That is all there is to it, but, as you can see, it is a two-man operation."

"But how do I—"

"Haste, haste! There are similar controls at the other end. You pull the lever, wait two minutes, enter the conveyor yourself. I will fetch you—if you are sure."

"I'm sure, dammit!"

"Remember, you go without training, without the opportunity everyone else has."

"You already told me that. Mars is half-way to eternity. Mars is limbo. If I can't go back to Earth I want to go— well, to Nowhere. There are too many ghosts here, too many memories with nothing to do."

Arkalion shrugged, entered the booth. "Pull the lever," he said, and shut the door.

Temple reached up, grasped the lever firmly in his hand, yanked it. It slid smoothly to the position marked "transport." Temple heard nothing, saw nothing, began to think the device, whatever it was, did not work. Did Arkalion somehow get *moved* inside the booth?

Temple thought he heard footfalls on the stairs outside. Soon, faintly, he could hear voices. Someone banged on the door to the hall. Licking dry lips, Temple opened the booth, peered inside.

Empty.

The voices clamored, fists pounded on the door. Something clicked. Tumblers fell. The door to the great, bright hall sprung outward. Someone rushed in at Temple, who met him savagely with a short, chopping blow to his jaw. The man, temporarily blinded by the dazzling light, stumbled back in the path of his fellows.

Temple darted into the booth, the conveyor, and slammed it shut. Fingers clawed on the outside.

A sound almost too intense to be heard rang in Temple's ears. He lost consciousness instantly.

CHAPTER VI

"WHAT A cockeyed world," said Alaric Arkalion Sr. to his son. "You certainly can't plan on anything, even if you do have more money than you'll ever possibly need in a lifetime."

"Don't feel like that," said young Alaric. "I'm not in prison any longer, am I?"

"No. But you're not free of the Nowhere Journey, either. There is an unheralded special trip to Nowhere, two weeks from today, I have been informed."

"Oh?"

"Yes, oh. I have also been informed that you will be on it. You didn't escape after all, Alaric."

"Oh. Oh!"

"What bothers me most is that scoundrel Smith somehow managed to escape. They haven't found him yet, I have also been informed. And since my contract with him calls for ten million dollars 'for services rendered,' I'll have to pay."

"But he didn't prevent me from—"

"I can't air this thing, Alaric! But listen, son: when you go where you are going, you're liable to find another Alaric Arkalion, your double. Of course, that would be Smith. If you can get him to cut his price in half because of what has happened, I would be delighted. If you could somehow manage to wring his neck, I would be even more delighted. Ten million dollars—for nothing."

"I'm so excited," murmured Mrs. Draper. Stephanie watched her on one of the new televiewers, recently installed in place of the telephone.

"What is it?"

"Our bill has been passed by a landslide majority in both houses of Congress!"

"Ooo!" cried Stephanie.

"Not very coherent, my dear, but those are my sentiments exactly. In two weeks there will be a Journey to Nowhere, a special one which will include, among its passengers, a woman."

"But the study which had to be made—?"

"It's already been made. From what I gather, they can't take it very far. Most of their conclusions had to be based on supposition. The important thing, though, is this: a woman *will* be sent. The way the C.E.L. figures it, my dear, is that a woman falling in the twenty-one to twenty-six age group should be chosen, a woman who meets all the requirements placed upon the young men."

"Yes," said Stephanie. "Of course. And I was just thinking that I would be—"

"Remember those chickens!" cautioned Mrs. Draper. "We already have one hundred seventy-seven volunteers who'd claw each other to pieces for a chance to go."

"Wrong," Stephanie said, smiling. "You now have one hundred seventy-eight."

"Room for only one, my dear. Only one, you know."

"Then cross the others off your list. I'm already packing my bag."

When Temple regained consciousness, it was with the feeling that no more than a split second of time had elapsed. So much had happened so rapidly that, until now, he hadn't had time to consider it.

Arkalion had vanished.

Vanished—he could use no other word. He was there, standing in the booth—and then he wasn't. Simple as that. Now you see it, now you don't. And goodbye, Arkalion.

But goodbye Temple, too. For hadn't Temple entered the same booth, waiting but a second until Arkalion activated the mechanism at the other end? And certainly Temple wasn't in the booth now. He smiled at the ridiculously simple logic of his thoughts. He stood in an open field, the blades of grass rising to his knees, as much brilliant purple as they were green. Waves of the grass, stirred like tide by the gentle wind, and hills rolling off toward the horizon in whichever direction he turned. Far away, the undulating hills lifted to a half soft mauve sky. A somber red sun with twice Sol's apparent disc but half its brightness hung midway between zenith and horizon completing the picture of peaceful other-worldliness.

Wherever this was, it wasn't Earth—or Mars.

Nowhere?

Temple shrugged, started walking. He chose his direction at random, crushing an easily discernible path behind him in the surprisingly brittle grass. The warm sun baked his back comfortably, the soft-stirring wind caressed his cheeks. Of Arkalion he found not a trace.

Two hours later Temple reached the hills and started climbing their gentle slopes. It was then that he saw the figure approaching on the run. It took him fully half a minute to realize that the runner was not human.

After months of weightless inactivity, things started to happen for Sophia. The feeling of weight returned, but weight as she never had felt it before. It was as if someone was sitting on every inch of her body, crushing her down. It made her gasp, forced her eyes shut and, although she could not see it, contorted her face horribly. She lost consciousness, coming to some time later with a dreadful feeling of loginess.

Someone swam into her vision dimly, stung her arm briefly with a needle. She slept.

She was on a table, stretched out, with lights glaring down at her. She heard voices.

"The new system is far better than testing, comrade."

"Far more efficient, far more objective. Yes."

"The brain emits electromagnetic vibration. Strange, is it not, that no one before ever imagined it could tell a story. A completely accurate story two years of testing could not give us."

"In Russia we have gone far with the biological, psychological sciences. The West flies high with physics. Give them Mars; bah, they can have Mars."

"True, Comrade. The journey to Jupiter is greater, the time consumed is longer, the cost, more expensive. But here on Jupiter we can do something they cannot do on Mars."

"I know."

"We can make supermen. Supermen, comrade. A wedding of Nietzsche and Marx."

"Careful. Those are dangerous thoughts."

"Merely an allusion, comrade. Merely a harmless allusion. But you take an ordinary human being and train him on Jupiter, speeding his time-sense and metabolic rate tremendously with certain endocrine secretions so that one day is as a month to him. You take him and subject him to big Jupiter's pull of gravity, more than twice Earth's—and in three weeks you have, yes—you have a superman."

"The woman wakes."

"Shh. Do not frighten her."

Sophia stretched, every muscle in her body aching. Slowly, as in a dream, she sat up. It required strength, the mere act of pulling her torso upright!

"What have you done to me?" she cried, focusing her still-dim vision on the two men.

"Nothing, comrade. Relax."

Sophia turned slowly on the table, got one long shapely leg draped over its edge.

"Careful, comrade."

What were they warning her about? She merely wanted to get up and stretch; perhaps then she would feel better. Her toe touched the floor, she swung her other leg over, aware of but ignoring her nakedness.

"A good specimen."

"Oh, yes, comrade. So this time they send a woman among the others. Well, we shall do our work. Look—see the way she is formed, so lithe, loose-limbed, agile. See the toning of the muscles? Her beauty will remain, comrade, but Jupiter shall make an amazon of her."

Sophia had both feet on the floor now. She was breathing hard, felt suddenly sick to her stomach. Placing both her hands on the table edge, she pushed off and staggered for two or three paces. She crumpled, buckling first at the knees then the waist and fell in a writhing heap.

"Pick her up."

Hands under her arms, tugging. She came off the floor easily, dimly aware that someone carried her hundred and thirty pounds effortlessly. "Put me down!" she cried. "I want to try again. I am crippled, crippled! You have crippled me . . ."

"Nothing of the sort, comrade. You are tired, weak, and Jupiter's gravity field is still too strong for you. Little by little, though, your muscles will strengthen to Jupiter's demands. Gravity will keep them from bulging, expanding; but every muscle fibre in you will have twice, three times its original strength. Are you excited?"

"I am tired and sick. I want to sleep. What is Jupiter?"

"Jupiter is a planet circling the sun at—never mind, comrade. You have much to learn, but you can assimilate it with much less trouble in your sleep. Go ahead, sleep."

Sophia retched, was sick. It had been years since she cried.

But naked, afraid, bewildered, she cried herself to sleep.

Things happened while she slept, many things. Certain en-
doctrine extracts accelerated her metabolism astonishingly.
Within half an hour her heart was pumping blood through
her body two hundred beats per minute. An hour later it
reached its full rate, almost one thousand contractions every
sixty seconds. All her other metabolic functions increased ac-
cordingly, and Sophia slept deeply for a week of subjective
time—in hours. The same machine which had gleaned everything from her mind far more accurately than a battery of
tests, a refinement of the electro-encephalogram, was now
played in reverse, giving back to Sophia everything it had
taken plus electrospool after electrospool of science, mathe-
matics, logic, economics, history (Marxian, these last two),
languages (including English), semantics and certain spec-
cialized knowledge she would need later on the Stalintrek.

Still sleeping, Sophia was bathed in a warm whirlpool of
soothing liquid; rubbed, massaged, her muscle-toning begun
while she rested and regained her strength. Three hours
later, objective time, she awoke with a headache and with
more thoughts spinning around madly inside her brain than
she ever knew existed. Gingerly, she tried standing again,
lifting herself nude and dripping wet from a tub of steaming
amber stuff. She stood, stretched, permitted her fright to
vanish with a quick wave of vertigo which engulfed her.
She had been fed intravenously, but a tremendous hunger
possessed her. Before eating, however, she was to find herself in a gymnasium, the air close and stifling. She was
massaged again, told to do certain exercises which seemed
simple but which she found extremely difficult, forced to
run until she thought she would collapse, with her legs, dragging like lead.

She understood, now. Somehow she knew she was on
Jupiter, the fifth and largest planet, where the force of
gravity is so much greater than on Earth that it is an effort

even to walk. She also knew that her metabolic rate had
been accelerated beyond all comprehension and that in a
comparatively short time—objective time—she would have
thrice her original strength. All this she knew without knowing how she knew, and that was the most staggering fact
of all. She did what her curt instructors bid, then dragged
her aching muscles and her headache into a dining room
where tired, forlorn-looking men sat around eating. Well
the food at least was good. Sophia attacked it ravenously.

It did not take Temple long to realize that the creature
running downhill at him, leaving a crushed and broken wake
in the purple and green grass, was not human. At first
Temple toyed with the idea of a man on horseback, for the
creature ran on four limbs and had two left over as arms.
Temple gaped.

The whole thing was one piece!

Centaur?

Hardly. Too small, for one thing. No bigger than a man,
despite the three pairs of limbs. And then Temple had
time to gape no longer, for the creature, whatever it was,
flashed past him at what he now had to consider a gallop.

More followed. Different. Temple stared and stared. One
could have been a great, sentient hoop, rolling downhill and
gathering momentum. If he carried the wheel analogy further, a huge eye stared at him from where the hub would
have been. Something else followed with kangaroo leaps. One
thick-thewed leg propelled it in tremendous, fifteen-foot
strides while its small, flapper-like arms beat the air pro-
digiously.

Legions of creatures. All fantastically different. *I'm going
crazy*, Temple thought, then said it aloud. "I'm going crazy."

Theorizing thus, he heard a whir overhead, whirled, looked
up. Something was poised a dozen feet off the ground, a
large, box-like object seven or eight feet across, rotors spin-

ning above it. That, at least, he could understand. A helicopter.

"I'm lowering a ladder, Kit. Swing aboard."

Arkalion's voice.

Stunned enough to accept anything he saw, Temple waited for the rope ladder to drop, grasped its end, climbed. He swung his legs over a sill, found himself in a neat little cabin with Arkalion, who hauled the ladder in and did something to the controls. They sped away. Temple had one quick moment of lucid thought before everything which had happened in the last few moments shoved logic aside. What he had observed looked for all the world like a footrace.

"Where the hell *are* we?" Temple demanded breathlessly.

Arkalion smiled. "Where do you think? Journey's end. Welcome to Nowhere, Kit. Welcome to the place where all your questions can be answered because there's no going back. Sorry I set you down in that field by mistake, incidentally. Those things sometimes happen."

"Can I just throw the questions at you?"

"If you wish. It isn't really necessary, for you will be indoctrinated when we get you over to Earth city where you belong."

"What do you mean, there's no going back? I thought they had a rotation system which for one reason or another wasn't practical at the moment. That doesn't sound like no going back, ever."

Arkalion grunted, shrugged. "Have it your way. I *know*."

"Sorry. Shoot."

"Just how far do you think you have come?"

"Search me. Some other star system, maybe?"

"Maybe. Clean across the galaxy, Kit."

Temple whistled softly. "It isn't something you can grasp just by hearing it. Across the galaxy . . ."

"That isn't too important just now. How long did you think the journey took?"

Temple nodded eagerly. "That's what gets me. It was amazing, Alaric. Really amazing. The whole trip couldn't have taken more than a moment or two. I don't get it. Did we slip out of normal space into some other—uh, continuum, and speed across the length of the galaxy like that?"

"The answer to your questions is yes. But your statement is way off. The journey did not take seconds, Kit."

"No? Instantaneous?"

"Far more than seconds. To reach here from Earth you traveled five thousand years."

"What?"

"More correctly, it was five thousand years ago that you left Mars. You would need a time machine to return, and there is no such thing. The Earth you know is the length of the galaxy and five thousand years behind you."

CHAPTER VII

IT COULD have been a city in New England, or maybe Wisconsin. Main Street stretched for half a mile from Town Hall to the small department store. Neon tubing brightened every store front, busy proprietors could be seen at work through the large plate glass windows. There was the bustle you might expect on any Main Street in New England or Wisconsin, but you could not draw the parallel indefinitely.

There were only men. No women.

The hills in which the town nestled were too purple—not purple with distance but the natural color of the grass.

A somber red sun hung in the pale mauve sky.

This was Earth City, Nowhere.

Arkalion had deposited Temple in the nearby hills, promised they would see one another again. "It may not be so soon," Arkalion had said, "but what's the difference? You'll spend the rest of your life here. You realize you are lucky, Kit. If you hadn't come, you would have been dead these five thousand years. Well, good luck."

Dead—five thousand years. The Earth as he knew it, dust. Stephanie, a fifty generation corpse. Nowhere was right. End of the universe.

Temple shuffled his feet, trudged on into town. A man passed him on the street, stooped, gray-haired. The man nodded, did a mild double-take. *I'm an unfamiliar face,* Temple thought.

"Howdy," he said. "I'm new here."

"That's what I thought, stranger. Know just about every-one in these here parts, I do, and I said to myself, now there's a newcomer. Funny you didn't come in the regular way."

"I'm here," said Temple.

"Yeah. Funny thing, you get to know everyone. Eh, what you say your name was?"

"Christopher Temple."

"Make it my business to know everyone. The neighborly way, I always say. Temple, eh? We have one here."

"One what?"

"Another fellow name of Temple. Jase Temple, son."

"I'll be damned!" Temple cried, smiling suddenly. "I will be damned. Tell me, old timer, where can I find him?"

"Might be anyplace. Town's bigger'n it looks. I tell you, though, Jase Temple's our co-ordinator. You'll find him there, the co-ordinator's office. Town Hall, down the end of the street."

"I already passed it," Temple told the man. "And thanks."

Temple's legs carried him at a brisk pace, past the row of store fronts and down to the Town Hall. He read a directory, climbed a flight of stairs, found a door marked:
JASON TEMPLE
Earth City Co-ordinator.
Heart pounding, Temple knocked, heard someone call, "Come in."
He pushed the door in and stared at his brother, just rising to face him.
"Kit! Kit! What are you doing . . . so you took the journey too!"
Jason ran to him, clasped his shoulders, pounded them. "You sure are looking fit. Kit, you could have knocked me over with half a feather, coming in like that."
"You're looking great too, Jase," Temple lied. He hadn't seen his brother in five years, had never expected to see him again. But he remembered a full-faced, smiling man somewhat taller than himself, somewhat broader across the shoulders. The Jason he saw looked forty-five or fifty but was hardly out of his twenties. He had fierce, smouldering eyes, gaunt cheeks, graying hair. He seemed a bundle of restless, nervous energy.
"Sit down, Kit. Start talking, kid brother. Start talking and don't stop till next week. Tell me everything. Everything! Tell me about the blue sky and the moon at night and the way the ocean looks on a windy day and . . ."
"Five years," said Temple. "Five years."
"Five thousand, you mean," Jason reminded him. "It hardly seems possible. How are the folks, Kit?"
"Mom's fine. Pop too. He's sporting a new Chambers Converto. You should see him, Jase. Sharp."
"And Ann?" Jason looked at him hopefully. Ann had been Jason's Stephanie—but for the Nowhere Journey they would have married.
"Ann's married," Temple said.

"Oh. Oh. That's swell, Kit. Really swell. I mean, what the hell, a girl shouldn't wait forever. I told her not to, anyway."

"She waited four years, then met a guy and—"

"A nice guy?"

"The best," said Temple. "You'd like him."

Temple saw the vague hurt come to Jason's smouldering eyes. Then it was the same. One part of Jason wanted her to remain his over an unthinkable gap, another part wanted her to live a good, full life.

"I'm glad," said Jason. "Can't expect a girl to wait without hope . . ."

"Then there's no hope we'll ever get back?"

Jason laughed harshly. "You tell me. Earth isn't merely sixty thousand light years away. Kit, do you know what a light year is?"

Temple said he thought he did.

"Sixty thousand of them. A dozen eternities. But the Earth we know is also dead. Dead five thousand years. The folks, Center City, Ann, her husband—all dust. Five thousand years old . . . Don't mind me, Kit."

"Sure. Sure, I understand." But Temple didn't, not really. You couldn't take five thousand years and chuck them out the window in what seemed the space of a heart beat and then realize they were gone permanently, forever. Not a period of time as long as all of recorded civilization—you couldn't take it, tack it on after 1992 and accept it. Somehow, Temple realized, the five thousand years were harder to swallow than the sixty thousand light years.

"Well," with a visible effort, Jason snapped out of his reverie. Temple accepted a cigarette gratefully, his first in a long time. *In fifty centuries*, he thought bitterly, burrowing deeper into a funk.

"Well," said Jason, "I'm acting like a prize boob. How selfish can I get? There must be an awful lot you'd like to know, Kit."

"That's all right. I was told I'd be indoctrinated."

"Ordinarily, you would. But there's no shipment now, none for another three months. Say, how the devil *did* you get here?"

"That's a long story. Nowhere Journey, same as you, with a little assist to speed things up on Mars. Jase, tell me this: what are we doing here? What is everyone doing here? What's the Nowhere Journey all about? What kind of a glorified foot-race did I see a while ago, with a bunch of creatures out of the telio science-fiction shows?"

Jason put his own cigarette out, changed his mind, lit another one. "Sort of like the old joke, where does an alien go to register?"

"Sort of."

"It's a big universe," said Jason, evidently starting at the beginning of something.

"I'm just beginning to learn *how* big!"

"It would be pretty unimaginative of mankind to consider itself the only sentient form of life, Earth the only home of intelligence, both from a scientific and a religious point of view. We kind of expected to find—neighbors out in space. Kit, the sky is full of stars, most stars have planets. The universe crawls with life, all sorts of life, all sorts of intelligent life. In short, we are not alone. It would be sort of like taking the jet-shuttle from Washington to New York during the evening rush and expecting to be the only one aboard. In reality, you're lucky to get breathing space.

"There are biped intelligences, like humans. There are radial intelligences, one-legged species, tall, gangling creatures, squat ones, pancake ones, giants, dwarfs. There are green skins and pink skins and coal black—and yes, no skins. There are . . . but you get the idea."

"Uh-huh."

"Strangely enough, most of these intelligences are on about the same developmental level. It's as if the Creator turned everything on at once, like a race, and said 'okay, guys get started.' Maybe it's because, as scientists figure, the whole universe got wound up and started working as a unit. I don't know. Anyway, that's the way it is. All the intelligences worth talking about are on about the same cultural level. Atomics, crude spaceflight, wars they can't handle.

"And this is interesting, Kit. Most of 'em are bipedal. Not really human, not fully human. You can see the difference. But seventy-five percent of the races I've encountered have had basic similarities. A case of the Creator trying to figure out the best of all possible life-patterns and coming up with this one. Offers a wide range for action, for adaptation, stuff like that. Anyway, I'm losing track of things."

"Take it easy. From what you tell me I have all the time in the world."

"Well, I said all the races are developmentally parallel. That's almost true. One of them is not. One of them is so far ahead that the rest of us have hardly reached the crawling stage by comparison. One of them is the Super Race, Kit.

"Their culture is old, incredibly old. So old, in fact, that some of us figure it's been hanging around since before the Universe took shape. Maybe that's why all the others are on one level, a few thousand million years behind the Super Race.

"So, take this Super Race. For some reason we can't understand, it seems to be on the skids. That's just figurative. Maybe it's dying out, maybe it wants to pack up and leave the galaxy altogether, maybe it's got other undreamed of business other undreamed of places. Anyway, it wants out. But it's got an eon-old storehouse of culture and maybe it figures someone ought to have access to that and keep the galaxy in running order. But who? That's the problem. Who gets all this information, a million million generations of scientific problems, all carefully worked out? Who, among all the parallel races on all the worlds of the Universe? That's quite a problem, even for our Super Race boys.

"You'd think they'd have ways to solve it, though. With calculating machines or whatever will follow calculating machines after Earthmen and all the others find the next faltering step after a few thousand years. Or with plain horse sense and logic, developed to a point—after millions of years at it—where it never fails. Or solve the problem with something we've never heard of, but solve it anyway."

"What's all this got to do with—? I mean, it's an interesting story and when I get a chance to digest it I'll probably start gasping, but what about Nowhere and . . ."

"I'm coming to that. Kit, what would you say if I told you that the most intelligent race the Universe has ever produced solves the biggest problem ever handed anyone—by playing games?"

"I'd say you better continue."

"That's the purpose of Nowhere, Kit. Every planet, every race has its Nowhere. We all come here and we play games. Planet with the highest score at the end of God knows how long wins the Universe, with all the science and the wisdom needed to fashion that universe into a dozen different kinds of heaven. And to decide all this, we play games.

"Don't get the wrong idea. I'm not complaining. If the Superboys say we play, then we play. I'd take their word for it if they told me I had fifteen heads. But it's the sort of thing which doesn't let you get much sleep. Oh, Earth has a right to be proud of its record. United North America is in second place on a competition that's as wide as the Universe. But we're not first. Second. And I have a hunch from what's been going on around here that the games are drawing to a close.

"Fantastic, isn't it? Out of thousands of entrants, we're good enough to place second. But some planet out near the star Deneb has us hopelessly outclassed. We might as well get the booby prize. They'll win and own the Universe—us included."

Jason had leaned forward as he spoke, and was sitting on the edge of his chair now. The room was comfortably cool, but sweat beaded his forehead, dripped from his chin.

Temple lit another cigarette, inhaling deeply. "You said the United States—North America—was second. I thought this was a planet-wide competition, planet against planet."

"Earth is the one exception I've been able to find. The Deneb planet heads the list, then comes North America. After that, the planet of a star I never heard of. In fourth place is the Soviet Union."

"I'll be damned," said Temple. "Well, okay. Mind if I store that away for future reference? I've got another question. What kind of—uh, games do we play?"

"You name it. Mental contests. Scientific problems to be worked out with laboratories built to our specifications. Emotional problems with scores of men driven neurotic or worse every year. Problems of adaptability. Responses to environmental challenge. Stamina contests. Tests of strength, of endurance. Tests to determine depths of emotion. Tests to determine objectivity in what should be an objective situation. But the way everything is organized it's almost like a giant-sized, never ending Olympic Games, complete with some cockeyed sports events too, by the way."

"With all the pageantry, too?"

"No. But that's another story."

"Anyway, what I saw *was* a foot-race! And sorry, Jase, but I have another question."

Jason shrugged, spread his hands wide.

"How come all this talk about rotation? It isn't possible, not with a fifty century gap."

"I know. They just let us in on that little deal a couple of years ago. Till then, we didn't know. We thought it was distance only. In time, after all this was over, we could go home. That's what we thought," Jason said bitterly. "Actually, it's twice five thousand years. Five to come here, five to return. Ten thousand years separate us from the Earth we know, and even if we could go home, that wouldn't be going home at all—to Earth ten thousand years in the future.

"Oh, they had us hoodwinked. Afraid we might say no or something. They never mentioned the length or duration of the trip. I don't understand it, none of us do and we have some top scientists here. Something to do with suspended animation, with contra-terrene matter, with teleportation, something about latent extra-sensory powers in everyone, about the ability to break down an object—or a creature or a man—to its component atoms, to reverse—that's the word, reverse—those atoms and send them spinning off into space as contra-terrene matter.

"It all boils down to putting a man in a machine on Mars, pulling a lever, materializing him here five thousand years later." Jason smiled with only a trace of humor. "Any questions?"

"About a thousand," said Temple. "I—"

Something buzzed on Jason's desk and Temple watched him pick up a microphone, say: "Co-ordinator speaking. What's up?"

The voice which answered, clear enough to be in the room with them and without the faintest trace of mechanical or electrical transfer, spoke in a strange, liquid-syllabled language Temple had never heard. Jason responded in the same language, with an apparent ease which surprised Temple—until he remembered that his brother had always had a knack of picking up foreign languages. Maybe that was why he held the Co-ordinator's job—whatever it was he co-ordinated.

There was fluency in the way Jason spoke, and alarm. The trouble-lines etched deeply on his face stood out sharply, his eyes, if possible, grew more intense. "Well," he said,

putting the mike down and staring at Temple without seeing him, "I'm afraid that does it."

"What's the trouble?"

"Everything."

"Anything I can do?"

"Item. The Superboys have discovered that Earth has
two contingents here—us and the Soviets. They're mad. Item.
Something will be done about it. Item. Soviet Russia has
made a suggestion, or that is, its people here. They will put
forth a champion to match one of our own choosing in the
toughest grind of all, something to do with responding to environmental challenge, which doesn't mean a hell of a lot
unless you happen to know something about it. Shall I go
on?"

And, when Temple nodded avidly. "We automatically
lose by default. One of the rules of that particular game is
that the contestant must be a newcomer. It's the sort of
game you have to know nothing about, and incidentally, it's
also the sort of game a man can get killed at. Well, the
Soviets have a whole contingent of newcomers to pick from.
We don't have any. As the Superboys see it, that's our own
tough luck. We lose by default."

"It seems to me—"

"How can anything 'seem to you?' You're new here . . .
I'm sorry Kit. What were you saying?"

"No. Go ahead."

"That's only the half of it. Right after Russia takes our
place and we're scratched off the list, the games go into
their final phase. That was the rumor all along, and it's just
been confirmed. Interesting to see what they do with all the
contestants *after* the games are over, after there's no more
Nowhere Journey."

"We could go back where we came from."

"Ten thousand years in the future?"

"I'm not afraid."

"Well, anyway, the Soviets put up a man, we can't match him. So it looks like the U.S.S.R. represents Earth officially. Not that it matters. We hardly have the chance of a very slushy snowball in a very hot hell. But still—"

"Our contestant, this guy who meets the Russians' challenge, has to be a newcomer?"

"That's what I said. Well, we can close up shop, I guess."

"You made a mistake. You said no newcomers have arrived. I'm here, Jase. I'm your man. Bring on your Russian Bear." Temple smiled grimly.

CHAPTER VIII

"You got to hand it to Temple's kid brother."

"Yeah. Cool as ice cubes."

"Are you guys kidding? He doesn't know what's in store for him, that's all."

"Do you?"

"Now that you mention it, no. Isn't a man here who can say for sure what kind of environmental challenges he'll have to respond to. Hypno-surgery sees to it the guys who went through the thing won't talk about it. As if that isn't security enough, the subject's got to be a brand new arrival!"

"Shh! Here he comes."

The brothers Temple entered Earth City's one tavern quietly, but on their arrival all the speculative talk subsided. The long bar, built to accommodate half a hundred pairs of elbows comfortably, gleamed with a luster unfamiliar to Temple. It might have been marble, but marble translucent rather than opaque, giving a beautiful three-dimensional effect to the surface patterns.

"What will it be?" Jason demanded.

"Whatever you're drinking is fine."

Jason ordered two scotches, neat, and the brothers drank. When Jason got a refill he started talking. "Does T.A.T. mean anything to you, Kit?"

"Tat? Umm—no. Wait a minute! T.A.T. Isn't that some kind of projective psychological test?"

"That's it. You're shown a couple of dozen pictures, more or less ambiguous, never cut and dry. Each one comes from a different stratum of the social environment, and you're told to create a dramatic situation, a story, for each picture. From your stories, for which you draw on your whole background as a human being, the psychometrician should be able to build a picture of your personality and maybe find out what, if anything, is bothering you."

"What's that to do with this response to environmental challenge thing?"

"Well," said Jason, drinking a third scotch, "the Super Boys have evolved T.A.T. to its ultimate. T.A.T.—that stands for Thematic Apperception Test. But in E.C.R.—environmental challenge and response, you don't see a picture and create a dramatic story around it. Instead, you get thrust into the picture, the situation, and you have to work out the solution—or suffer whatever consequences the particular environmental challenge has in store for you."

"I think I get you. But it's all make believe, huh?"

"That's the hell of it," Jason told him. "No, it's not. It is and it isn't. I don't know."

"You make it perfectly clear," Temple smiled. "The redheaded boy combed his brown hair, wishing it weren't blond."

Jason shrugged. "I'm sorry. For reasons you already know, the E.C.R. isn't very clear to me—or to anyone. You're not actually in the situation in a physical sense, but it can affect you physically. You *feel* you're there, you actually live everything that happens to you, getting injured if an injury occurs . . . and dying if you get killed. It's permanent, although you might actually be sleeping at the time. So whether it's real or not is a question for philosophy. From your point of view, from the point of view of someone going through it, it's real."

"So I become part of this—uh, game in about an hour."

"Right. You and whoever the Russians offer as your competition. No one will blame you if you want to back out, Kit; from what you tell me, you haven't even been adequately trained on Mars."

"If you draw on the entire background of your life for this E.C.R., then you don't need training. Shut up and stop worrying. I'm not backing out of anything."

"I didn't think you would, not if you're still as much like your old man as you used to be. Kit . . . good luck."

The fact that the technicians working around him were Earthmen permitted Temple to relax a little. Probably, it was planned that way, for entering the huge white cube of a building and ascending to the twelfth level on a moving ramp Temple had spotted many figures, not all of them human. If he had been strapped to the table by unfamiliar aliens, if the scent of alien flesh—or non-flesh—had been strong in the room, if the fingers—or appendages—which greased his temples and clamped an electrode to each one had not felt like human fingers, if the men talking to him had spoken in voices too harsh or too sibilant for human vocal chords— if all that had been the case whatever composure still remained his would have vanished.

"I'm Dr. Olson," said one white-gowned figure. "If any injuries occur while you lie here, I'm permitted to render first aid."

"The same for limited psychotherapy," said a shorter, heav-

ier man. "Though a fat lot of good it does when we never
know what's bothering you, and don't have the time to work
on it even if we did know."

"In short," said a third man who failed to identify himself,
"you may consider yourself as the driver of one of those
midget rocket racers. Do they still have them on Earth?
Good. You are the driver, and we here in this room are the
mechanics waiting in your pit. If anything goes wrong, you
can pull out of the race temporarily and have it repaired.
But in this particular race there is no pulling out: all repairs
are strictly of a first-aid nature and must be done while you
continue whatever you are doing. If you break your finger
and find a splint appearing on it miraculously, don't say you
weren't warned."

"Best of luck to you, young man," said the psycho-therapist.

"Here we go," said the doctor, finding the large vein on the
inside of Temple's forearm and plunging a needle into it.

Temple's senses whirled instantly, but as his vision clouded
he thought he saw a large, complex device swing down from
the ceiling and bathe his head in warming radiation. He
blinked, squinted, could see nothing but a swirling, cloudy
opacity.

Approximately two seconds later, Sophia Androvna Petrovitch watched as the white-gowned comrade tied a rubber
strap around her arm, waited for the vein to swell with
blood, then forced a needle in through its thick outer layer.
Was that a nozzle overhead? No, rather a lens, for from it
came amber warmth . . . which soon faded, with everything
else, into thick, churning fog . . .

Temple was abruptly aware of running, plunging headlong
and blindly through the fiercest storm he had ever seen.
Gusts of wind whipped at him furiously. Rain cascaded down
in drenching torrents. Foliage, brambles, branches struck
against his face; mud sucked at his feet. Big animal shapes

lumbered by in the green gloom, as frightened by the storm as was Temple.

His head darted this way and that, his eyes could see the gnarled tree trunks, the dense greenery, the lianas, creepers and vines of a tropical rain forest—but dimly. Green murk swirled in like thick smoke with every gust of wind, with the rain obscuring vision almost completely.

Temple ran until his lungs burned and he thought he must exhale fire. His leaden feet fought the mud with growing difficulty for every stride he took. He ran wildly and in no set direction, convinced only that he must find shelter or perish. Twice he crashed bodily into trees, twice stumbled to his knees only to pull himself upright again, sucking air painfully into his lungs and cutting out in a fresh direction.

He ran until his legs balked. He fell, collapsing first at the knees, then the waist, then flopping face down in the mud. Something prodded his back as he fell and reaching behind him weakly Temple was aware for the first time that a bow and a quiver of arrows hung suspended from his shoulders by a strong leather thong. He wore nothing but a loin cloth of some nameless animal skin and he wondered idly if he had slain the animal with the weapon he carried. Yet when he tried to recollect he found he could not. He remembered nothing but his frantic flight through the rain forest, as if all his life he had run in a futile attempt to leave the rain behind him.

Now as he lay there, the mud sucking at his legs, his chest, his armpits, he could not even remember his name. Did he have one? Did he have a life before the rain forest? Then why did he forget?

A sense not fully developed in man and called intuition by those who fail to understand it made him prop his head up on his hands and squint through the downpour. There was something off there in the foliage . . . someone . . .

A woman.

Temple's breath caught in his throat sharply. The woman
stood half a dozen paces off, observing him coolly with hands
on flanks. She stood tall and straight despite the storm and
from trim ankles to long, lithe legs to flaring loin-clothed hips,
to supple waist and tawny skin of fine bare breasts and
shoulders, to proud, haughty face and long dark hair loose
in the storm and glistening with rain, she was magnificent.
Her long, bronzed body gleamed with wetness and Temple
realized she was tall as he, a wild beautiful goddess of the
jungle. She was part of the storm and he accepted her
—but strangely, with the same fear the storm evoked. She
would make a lover the whole world might relish (what
world, Temple thought in confusion?) but she would make
a terrible foe.

And foe she was . . .

"I want your bow and arrows," she told him.

Temple wanted to suggest they share the weapon, but
somehow he knew in this world which was like a dream and
could tell him things the way a dream would and yet was
vividly real, that the woman would share nothing with anybody.

"They are mine," Temple said, climbing to his knees. He
remembered the animal-shapes lumbering by in the storm
and he knew that he and the animals would both stalk prey
when the storm subsided and he would need the bow and
arrows.

The woman moved toward him with a liquid motion beautiful to behold, and for the space of a heartbeat Temple
watched her come. "I will take them," she said.

Temple wasn't sure if she could or not, and although she
was a woman he feared her strangely. Again, it was as if
something in this dream-world real-world could tell him
more than he should know.

Making up his mind, Temple sprang to his feet, whirled
about and ran. He was plunging through the wild storm once

more, blinded by the occasional flashes of jagged green lightning, deafened by the peals of thunder which followed. And he was being pursued.

Minutes, hours, more than hours—for an eternity Temple ran. A reservoir of strength he never knew he possessed provided the energy for each painful step and running through the storm seemed the most natural thing in the world to him. But there came a time when his strength failed, not slowly, but with shocking suddenness. Temple fell, crawled a ways, was still.

It took him minutes to realize the storm no longer buffeted him, more minutes to learn he had managed to crawl into a cave. He had no time to congratulate himself on his good fortune, for something stirred outside.

"I am coming in," the woman called to him from the green murk.

Temple strung an arrow to his bow, pulled the string back and faced the cave's entrance squatting on his heels. "Then your first step shall be your last. I'll shoot to kill." And he meant it.

Silence from outside. Deafening.

Temple felt sweat streaming under his armpits; his hands were clammy, his hands trembled.

"You haven't seen the last of me," the woman promised. After that, Temple knew she was gone. He slept as one dead.

When Temple awoke, bright sunlight filtered in through the foliage outside his cave. Although the ground was a muddy ruin, the storm had stopped. Edging to the mouth of the cave, Temple spread the foliage with his hands, peered cautiously outside. Satisfied, he took his bow and arrows and left the cave, pangs of hunger knotting his stomach painfully.

The cave had been weathered in the side of a short, steep abutment a dozen paces from a gushing, swollen stream. Temple followed the course of the stream as it twisted through the jungle, ranging half a mile from his cave until the water course widened to form a water-hole. All morning Temple waited there, crouching in the grass, until one by one, the forest animals came to drink. He selected a small hare-like thing, notched an arrow to his bow, let it fly.

The animal jumped, collapsed, began to slink away into the undergrowth, dragging the arrow from its hindquarters. Temple darted after it, caught it in his hands and bashed its life out against the bole of a tree. Returning to his cave he found two flinty stones, shredded a fallen branch and nursed the shards dry in the strong sunlight. Soon he made a fire and ate.

In the days which followed, Temple returned to the water-hole and bagged a new catch every time he ventured forth. Things went so well that he began to range further and further from his cave exploring. Once however, he returned early to the water-hole and found footprints in the soft mud of its banks.

The woman.

That she had been observing him while he had hunted had never occurred to Temple, but now that the proof lay clearly before his eyes, the old feeling of uncertainty came back. And the next day, when he crept stealthily to the water-hole and saw the woman squatting there in the brush, waiting for him, he fled back to his cave.

The thought hit him suddenly. If she were stalking him, why must he flee as from his own shadow? There would be no security for either of them until either one or the other were gone—and gone meant dead. Then Temple would do his own stalking.

For several nights Temple hardly slept. He could have found the water-hole blindfolded merely by following the stream. Each night he would reach the hole and work, digging with a sharp stone, until he had fashioned a pit fully ten feet deep and six feet across. This he covered with branches, twigs, leaves and finally dirt.

When he returned in the morning he was satisfied with his work. Unless the woman made a careful study of the area, she would never see the pit. All that day Temple waited with his back to the water-hole, facing the camouflaged pit, the trap he had set, but the woman failed to appear. When she also did not come on the second day, he began to think his plan would not work.

The third day, Temple arrived with the sun, sat as before in the tall grass between the pit and the water-hole and waited. Several paces beyond his hidden trap he could see the tall trees of the jungle with vines and creepers hanging from their branches. At his back, a man's length behind him was the water-hole, its deepest waters no more than waist-high.

Temple waited until the sun stood high in the sky, then was fascinated as a small antelope minced down to the water-hole for a drink. *You'll make a fine breakfast tomorrow, he thought, smiling.*

Something, that strange sixth sense again, made Temple turn around and stand up. He had time for a brief look, a hoarse cry.

The woman had been the cleverer. She had set the final trap. She stood high up on a branch of one of the trees beyond the hidden pit and for an instant Temple saw her fine figure clearly, naked but for the loincloth. Then the soft curves became spring-steel.

The woman arched her body there on the high branch, grasping a stout vine and rocking back with it. Temple raised his bow, set an arrow to let it fly. But by then, the woman was in motion.

Long and lithe and graceful, she swung down on her vine,

gathering momentum as she came. Her feet almost brushed the lip of Temple's pit at the lowest arc of her flight, but she clung to the vine and it began to swing up again like a pendulum—toward Temple.

At the last moment he hunched his shoulder and tried to raise his arms for protection. The woman was quicker. She gathered her legs up under her, still clutching the vine with her slim, strong hands. The vine's arc carried her up at him; her knees were at a level with his head and she brought them up savagely, close together striking Temple brutally at the base of his jaw. Temple screamed as his head was jerked back with terrible force.

The bow flew from his fingers and he fell into the waterhole, flat on his back.

Sophia let the vine carry her out over the water, then dropped from it. Waist deep, she waded to where the man lay, unconscious on his back, half in, half out of the shallowest part of the water. She reached him, prodded his chest with her foot. When he did not stir, she rocked her weight down gracefully on her long leg, forcing his head under water. With a haughty smile, she watched the bubbles rise . . .

In the small room where Temple's body lay in repose on a table the white-smocked doctor looked at the psychotherapist questioningly. "What's happening?"

"Can't tell, doctor. But—"

Suddenly Temple's still body rocked convulsively, his neck stretched, his head shot up and back. Blood trickled from his mouth.

The doctor thrust out expert hands, examined Temple's jaw dexterously.

"Broken?" the psychotherapist demanded in a worried voice.

"No. Dislocated. He looks like he's been hit by a sledge

hammer, wherever he is now, whatever's happening. This E.C.R. is the damndest thing."

Temple's still form shuddered convulsively. He began to gasp and cough, obviously fighting for breath. An ugly blue swelling had by now lumped the base of his jaw.

"What's happening?" demanded the psychotherapist.

"I can't be sure," said the doctor, shaking his head. "He seems to have difficulty in breathing . . . it's as if he were—drowning."

"Bad. Anything we can do?"

"No. We wait until this particular sequence ends." The doctor examined Temple again. "If it doesn't end soon, this man will die of asphyxiation."

"Call it off," the psychotherapist pleaded. "If he dies now Earth will be represented by Russia. Call it off!"

Someone entered the room. "*I* have the authority," he said, selecting a hypodermic from the doctor's rack and piercing the skin of Temple's forearm with it. "This first test has gone far enough. The Russian entry is clearly the winner, but Temple must live if he is to compete in another."

The racking convulsions which shook Temple's body subsided. He ceased his choking, began to breathe regularly. With grim swiftness, the doctor went to work on Temple's dislocated jaw while the man who had stopped the contest rendered artificial respiration.

The man was Alaric Arkalion.

The Comrade Doctor was exultant. "Jupiter training, comrade, has given us a victory."

"How can you be sure?"

"Our entrant is unharmed, the contest has been called. Wait . . . she is coming to."

Sophia stretched, rubbed her bruised knees, sat up.

"What happened, Comrade?" the doctor demanded.

"My knees ache," said Sophia, rubbing them some more.

"I—I killed him, I think. Strange, I never dreamed it would be that real."

"In a sense, it *was* real. If you killed the American, he will stay dead."

"Nothing mattered but that world we were in, a fantastic place. Now I remember everything, all the things I couldn't remember then."

"But your—ah, dream—what happened?"

Sophia rubbed her bruised knees a third time, ruefully. "I knocked him unconscious with these. I forced his head under water and drowned him. But—before I could be sure I finished the job—I came back . . . Funny that I should want to kill him without compunction, without reason." Sophia frowned, sat up. "I don't think I want anymore of this."

The doctor surveyed her coldly. "This is your task on the Stalintrek. This you will do."

"I killed him without a thought."

"Enough. You will rest and get ready for the second contest."

"But if he's dead—"

"Apparently he's not, or we would have been informed, Comrade Petrovitch."

"That is true," agreed the second man, who had remained silent until now. "Prepare for another test, Comrade."

Sophia was on the point of arguing again. After all it wasn't fair. If in the dream-worlds which were not dream worlds she was motivated by but one factor and that to destroy the American and if she faced him with the strength of her Jupiter training it would hardly be a contest. And now that she could think of the American without the all-consuming hatred the dream world had fostered in her, she realized he had been a pleasant-looking young man, quite personable, in fact. *I could like him,* Sophia thought and hoped fervently she had not drowned him. Still, if she had volunteered for the Stalintrek and this was the job they assigned her . . .

"I need no rest," she told the doctor, hardly trusting herself, for she realized she might change her mind. "I am ready any time you are.

CHAPTER IX

His NAME was Temple and it was the year 1960.

Christopher Temple had problems. He had his own life, too, which had nothing to do with the life of the real Christopher Temple, departed thirty-odd years later on the Nowhere Journey. Or rather, this *was* Christopher Temple, living his second E.C.R.. . . . Temple who had lost once, and who, if he lost again, would take the dreams and hopes of the Western world down into the dust of defeat with him. But as the fictional (although in a certain sense, real) Christopher Temple of 1960, he knew nothing of this.

The world could go to pot. The world was going to pot, anyway. Temple shuddered as he poured a fourth Canadian, downing it in a tasteless, burning gulp. Temple was a thermonuclear engineer with government subsidized degrees from three universities including the fine new one at Desert Rock. Temple was a thermo-nuclear engineer with top-secret government clearance. Temple was a thermo-nuclear engineer with more military secrets buzzing around inside his head than in a warehouse of burned Pentagon files.

Temple was also a thermo-nuclear engineer whose wife spied for the Russians.

He'd found out quite by accident, not meaning to eavesdrop at all. Returning home early one afternoon because the production engineer called a halt while further re-search was done on certain unstable isotopes, Temple was surprised to find his wife had a gentleman caller. He heard their voices clearly from where he stood out in the sun-parlor, and for a ridiculous instant he was torn between slinking upstairs and ignoring them altogether or barging into the living room like a high school boy flushed with jealousy. The mature thing to do, of course, was neither, and Temple was on the point of walking politely into the living room, saying hello and waiting for an introduction, when snatches of the conversation stopped him cold.

"Silly Charles! Kit doesn't suspect a thing. I would *know*."

"How can you be sure?"

"Intuition."

"On a framework of intuition you would place the fate of Red Empire?"

"Empire, Charles?" Temple could picture Lucy's raised eyebrow. He listened now, hardly breathing. For one wild moment he thought he would retreat upstairs and forget the whole thing. Life would be much simpler that way. A meaningless surrender to unreality, however, and it couldn't be done.

"Yes, Empire. Oh, not the land-grabbing, slave-dominating sort of things the Imperialists used to attempt, but a more subtle and hence more enduring empire. Let the world call us Liberator, we shall have Empire."

Lucy laughed, a sound which Temple loved. "You may keep your ideology, Charles. Play with it, bathe in it, get drunk on it or drown yourself in it. I want my money."

"You are frank."

Temple could picture Lucy's shrug. "I am a paid, professional spy. By now you have most of the information you need. I shall have the rest tonight."

'I'll see you in hell first!" Temple cried in rage, stalking into the room and almost smiling in spite of the situation when he realized how melodramatic his words must sound.

"Kit! Kit . . ." Lucy raised hand to mouth, then backed away flinching as if she had been struck.

"Yeah, Kit. A political cuckold, or does Charles get other services from you as well?"

"Kit, you don't . . ."

The man named Charles motioned for silence. Dapper, clean-cut, good-looking except for a surly, pouting mouth, he was a head shorter than either Temple or Lucy. "Don't waste your words, Sophia. Temple overheard us."

Sophia? thought Temple. "Sophia?" he said.

Charles nodded coolly. "The real Mrs. Temple was observed, studied, her every habit and whim catalogued by experts. A plastic surgeon, a psychologist, a sociologist, a linguist, a whole battery of experts molded Sophia here into a new Mrs. Temple. I must congratulate them, for you never suspected."

"Lucy?" Temple demanded dully. Reason stood suspended in a limbo of objective acceptance and subjective disbelief.

"Mrs. Temple was eliminated. Regrettable because we don't deal in senseless mayhem, but necessary."

Temple was not aware of leaving limbo until he felt the bruising contact of his knuckles with Charles' jaw. The short man toppled, fell at his feet. "Get up!" Temple cried, then changed his mind and tensed himself to leap upon the prone figure.

"Hold it," Charles told him quietly, wiping blood from his lips with one hand, drawing an automatic from his pocket with the other. "You'd better freeze, Temple. You die if you don't."

Temple froze, watched Charles slither away across the high-piled green carpet until, safely away across the room, he came upright groggily. He turned to the dead Lucy's double. "What do you think, Sophia?"

"I don't know. We could get out of here, probably get along without the final information."

"That isn't what I mean. Naturally, we'll never receive the final facts. I mean, what do you think about Temple?"

Sophia said she didn't know.

"Left alone, he would go to the police. Kidnapped, he would be worse than useless. Harmful, actually, for the authorities would suspect something. Even worse if we killed him. The point is, we don't want the authorities to think Temple gave information to anybody."

"Gave is hardly the word," said Sophia. "I was a good wife, but also a good gleaner. One hundred thousand dollars, Charles."

"You bitch," Temple said.

"Later," Charles told the woman. "The solution is this, Sophia: we must kill Temple, but it must look like suicide."

Sophia frowned in pretty concern. "Do we have to . . . kill him?"

"What's the matter, my dear? Have you been playing the wifely role too long? If Temple stands in the way of Red Empire, Temple must die."

Temple edged forward.

"Uh-uh," said Charles, "mustn't." He waved the automatic and Temple subsided.

"Is that right?" Sophia demanded. "Well, you listen to me. I have nothing to do with your Red Empire. I fled the Iron Curtain, came here to live voluntarily—"

"Do you really think it was on a voluntary basis that you went? We allowed you to go, Sophia. We encouraged it. That way, the job of our technicians was all the simpler. Whether you like it or not, you have been a cog in the machine of Red Empire."

"I still don't see why he has to die."

"Leave thinking to those who can. You have a smile, a

body, a certain way with men. I will think. I think that Temple should die."

"I don't," Sophia said.

"We're delaying needlessly. The man dies." And Charles raised his automatic, sufficiently irked to forget his suicide plan.

A gap of eight or nine feet separated the two men. It might as well have been infinity– and it would be soon, for Temple. He saw Charles' small hand tighten about the automatic, saw the trigger finger grow white. The weapon pointed at a spot just above his navel and briefly he found himself wondering what it would feel like for a slug to rip into his stomach, burning a path back to his spine. He decided to make the gesture at least, if he could do no more. He would jump for Charles.

Sophia beat him to it—and because Lucy was dead and Sophia looked exactly like her and Temple could not quite accept the fact, it seemed the most natural thing in the world. Cat-quick, Sophia leaped upon Charles' back and they went down together in a twisting thrashing tangle of arms and legs.

Temple did not wait for an invitation. He launched himself down after them, and then things began to happen . . . fast.

Sophia rolled clear, rose to her hands and knees, panting. Charles sat up cursing, nursing a badly scratched face. Temple hurtled at him, stretched him on his back again, began to pound hard fists into his face.

Charles did not have the automatic. Neither did Temple.

Something exploded against the back of Temple's head violently, throwing him off Charles and tumbling him over. Dimly he saw Sophia following through, the automatic in her hand, butt foremost. Temple's senses reeled. He tried to rise, succeeded only in a kind of shuddering slither before he subsided. He wavered between consciousness and uncon-

sciousness, heard as in a dream snatches of conversation.
"Shoot him . . . shoot him!"
"Shut up . . . I have . . . gun . . .go to hell."
". . . kill . . . only way."
"My way is different . . . out of here . . . discuss later."
". . . feel . . ."
"I said . . . out of here . . ."
The voices became a meaningless liquid torrent cascading
into a black pit.

Now Temple sat with a water-glass a third full of Canadian
in his hand, every once in a while reaching up gingerly to
explore the bruised swelling on his head, the blood-matted
hair which covered it. To be a cuckold was one thing, but
to be the naive, political pawn sort of cuckold who is not a
cuckold at all, he told himself, is for worse. To live with his
woman, eat the meals she cooked for him, talk to her, think
she understood him, sympathize with him, to make love
to her with passion while she responds with play-acting for
a hundred thousand dollar salary was suddenly the most
emasculating thing in the world for Temple. He had not
thought to ask how long it had been going on. Better,
perhaps, if he never knew. And somewhere lost in the maze
of his thoughts was the grimmest, bleakest reality of them
all: Lucy was dead. Lucy—dead. But where did Lucy leave
off, where did Sophia begin? Was Lucy dead that night
they returned more than a little drunk from the Chamber's
party, that night they danced in the living room until dawn
obscured the stars and he carried Lucy upstairs. Lucy or
Sophia? And the day they motored to the lake, their secret
lake, hardly more than a dammed, widened stream and
dreamed of the things they could do when the Cold War
ended? Lucy—or Sophia? Had he ever noticed a difference in
the way Lucy-Sophia cooked, in the way she spoke, the way
she let him make love to her? He thought himself into a

man-sized headache and found no answers. This way at least
the loss of his wife was not as traumatic as it might have
been. He knew not when she died or how and, in fact, Lucy-
Sophia seemed so much like the real thing that he did not
know where he could stop loving and start hating.

And the girl, the Russian girl, had saved his life. Why? He
couldn't answer that one either, unless if it were as Charles
suggested: Sophia had studied Lucy so carefully, had learned
her likes and dislikes, her wants and desires, had memorized
and practised every quirk of her character to such an extent
that Sophia was Lucy in essence.

Which, Temple thought, would make it all the harder to
seek out Sophia and kill her.

That was the answer, the only answer. Temple felt a dull
ache where his heart should have been, a pressure, a pounding, an unpleasant, unfamiliar lack of feeling. If he took his
story to the F.B.I. he had no doubt that Charles, Sophia
and whoever else worked this thing with them would be
caught, but he, Temple, would find himself with a lifelong,
unslakable emotional thirst. He had to quench it now and
then feel sorry so that he might heal. He had to quench it
with Sophia's blood . . . alone.

He found her a week later at their lake. He had looked
everywhere and had about given up, almost, in fact, ready
to turn his story over to the police But he had to think and
their lake was the place for that.

Apparently Sophia had the same idea. Temple parked
on the highway half a mile from their lake, made his way
slowly through the woods, golden dappled with sunlight.
He heard the waters gushing merrily, heard the sounds of
some small animal rushing off through the woods. He saw
Sophia.

She lay on their sunning rock in shorts and halter, completely relaxed, an opened magazine face down on the rock

beside her, a pair of sunglasses next to it. She had one knee up, one leg stretched out, one forearm shielding her eyes from the sun, one arm down at her side. Seeing her thus, Temple felt the pressure of his automatic in its holster under his arm. He could draw it out, kill her before she was aware of his presence. Would that make him feel better? Five minutes ago, he would have said yes. Now he hesitated. Kill her, who seemed as completely Lucy as he was Temple? Send a bullet ripping through the body which he had known and loved, or the body that had seemed so much like it he had failed to tell the difference?

Murder—Lucy?

"No," he said aloud. "Her name is Sophia."

The girl sat up, startled. "Kit," she said.

"Lucy."

"You can't make up your mind, either." She smiled just like Lucy.

Dumbly, he sat down next to her on the rock. Strong sunlight had brought a fine dew of perspiration to the bronzed skin of her face. She got a pack of cigarettes out from under the magazine, lit one, offered it to Temple, lit another and smoked it. "Where do we go from here?" she wanted to know.

"I—"

"You came to kill me, didn't you? Is that the only way you can ever feel better, Kit?"

"I—" He was going to deny it, then think.

"Don't deny it. Please." She reached in under his jacket, withdrawing her hand with the snub-nosed automatic in it. "Here," she said, giving it to him.

He took the gun, hefted it, let it fall, clattering, on the rock.

"Listen," she said. "I could have told you I was Lucy. If I said now that I am Lucy and if I kept on saying it, you'd believe me. You'd believe me because you'd want to."

"Well," said Temple.

"I am not Lucy. Lucy is dead. But . . . but I was Lucy in everything but being Lucy. I thought her thoughts, dreamed her dreams, loved her loves."

"You killed her."

"No. I had nothing to do with that. She was killed, yes. Not by me. Kit, if I asked you when Lucy stopped, and . . . when I began, could you tell me?"

He had often thought about that. "No," he said truthfully. "You're as much my wife as—she was."

She clutched at his hand impulsively. Then, when he failed to respond, she withdrew her own hand. "Then—then I *am* Lucy. If I am Lucy in every way, Lucy never died."

"You betrayed me. You stood by while murder was committed. You are guilty of espionage."

"Lucy loved you. I am Lucy . . ."

". . . Betrayed me . . ."

"For a hundred thousand dollars. For the chance to live a normal life, for the chance to forget Leningrad in the wintertime, watery potato soup, rags for clothing, swaggering commissars, poverty, disease. Do you think I realized I could fall in love with you so completely? If I did, don't you think that would have changed things? I am not Sophia, Kit. I was, but I am not. They made me Lucy. Lucy can't be dead, not if I am she in every way."

"What can we do?"

"I don't know. I only want to be your wife . . ."

"Well, then tell me," he said bitterly. "Shall I go back to the plant and continue working, knowing all the time that our most closely guarded secret is in Russian hands and that my wife is responsible?" He laughed. "Shall I do that?"

"Your secrets never went anywhere."

"Shall I . . . *what?*"

"Your secrets never went anywhere. Charles is dead. I have destroyed all that we took. I am not Russian any

longer. American. They made me American. They made me
Lucy. I want to go right on being Lucy, your wife."

Temple said nothing for a long time. He realized now he
could not kill her. But everything else she suggested . . .
"Tell me," he said. "Tell me, how long have you been
Lucy? You've got to tell me that."

"How long have we been married?"

"You know how long. Three years."

Sophia crushed her cigarette out on the rock, wiped perspiration (tears?) from her cheek with the back of her
hand. "You have never known anyone but me in your
marriage bed, Kit."

"You—you're lying."

"No. They did what they did on the eve of your marriage. I have been your wife for as long as you have had
one."

Temple's head whirled. It had been a quick courtship. He
had known Lucy only two weeks in those hectic post-graduate
days of 1957. But for fourteen brief days, it was Sophia he
had known all along.

"Sophia, I—"

"There is no Sophia, not any more."

He had hardly known Lucy, the real Lucy. This girl here
was his wife, always had been. Had the first fourteen days
with Lucy been anything but a dream? He was sorry Lucy
had died—but the Lucy he had thought dead was Sophia,
very much alive.

He took her in his arms, almost crushing her. He held her
that way, kissed her savagely, letting passion of a different
sort take the place of murder.

This is my woman, he thought, and awoke on his white
pallet in Nowhere.

"I am awake," said Temple.

"We see that. You shouldn't be."

"No?"

"No. There is one more dream."

Temple dozed restfully but was soon aware of a commotion. Strangely, he did not care. He was too tired to open his eyes, anyway. Let whatever was going to happen, happen. He wanted his sleep.

But the voice persisted.

"This is highly irregular. You came in here once and—"

"I did you a favor, didn't I?" (That voice is familiar, Temple thought.)

"Well, yes. But what now?"

"Temple's record is now one and one. In the second sequence he was the victor. The Soviet entry had to extract certain information from him and turn it over to her people. She extracted the information well enough but somehow Temple made her change her mind. The information never went anyplace. How Temple managed to play counterspy I don't know, but he played it and won."

"That's fine. But what do you want?"

"The final E.C.R. is critical." (The voice was Arkalion's!) "How critical, I can't tell you. Sufficient though, if you know that you lose no matter how Temple fares. If the Russian woman defeats Temple, you lose."

"Naturally."

"Let me finish. If Temple defeats the Russian woman, you also lose. Either way, Earth is the loser. I haven't time to explain what you wouldn't understand anyway. Will you cooperate?"

"Umm-mm. You did save Temple's life. Umm-mm, yes. All right."

"The third dream sequence is the wrong dream, the wrong contest with the wrong antagonist at the wrong time, when a far more important contest is brewing . . . with the fate of Earth as a reward for the victor."

"What do you propose?"

"I will arrange Temple's final dream. But if he disappears from this room, don't be alarmed. It's a dream of a different sort. Temple won't know it until the dream progresses, you won't know it until everything is concluded, but Temple will fight for a slave or a free Earth."

"Can't you tell us more?"

"There is no time, except to say that along with the rest of the Galaxy, you've been duped. The Nowhere Journey is a grim, tragic farce.

"Awaken, Kit!"

Temple awoke into what he thought was the third and final dream. Strange, because this time he knew where he was and why, knew also that he was dreaming, even remembered vividly the other two dreams.

"Stealth," said Arkalion, and led Temple through long, white-walled corridors. They finally came to a partially open door and paused there. Peering within, Temple saw a room much like the one he had left, with two white-gowned figures standing anxiously over a table. And prone on the table was Sophia, whom Temple had loved short moments before, in his second dream. Moments? Years. (Never, except in a dream.)

"She's lovely," Arkalion whispered.

"I know." Like himself, Sophia was garbed in a loose jumper and slacks.

"Stealth," said Arkalion again. "Haste." Arkalion disappeared.

"Well," Temple told himself. "What now? At least in the other dreams I was thrust so completely into things, I knew what to do." He rubbed his jaw grimly. "Not that it did much good the first time."

Temple poked the partially-ajar door with his foot, pushing it open. The two white-smocked figures had their backs to him, leaned intently over the table and Sophia. Without knowing what motivated him, Temple leaped into the room, grasped the nearer figure's arm, whirled him around. Startled confusion began to alter the man's coarse features, but his face went slack when Temple's fist struck his jaw with terrible strength. The man collapsed.

The second man turned, mouthing a stream of what must have been Russian invective. He parried Temple's quick blow with his left hand, crossing his own right fist to Temple's face and almost ending the fight as quickly as it had started. Temple went down in a heap and was vaguely aware of the Russian's booted foot hovering over his face. He reached out, grabbed the boot with both hands, twisted. The man screamed and fell and then they were rolling over and over, striking each other with fists, knees, elbows, gouging, butting, cursing. Temple found the Russian's throat, closed his hands around it, applied pressure. Fists pounded his face, nails raked him, but slowly he succeeded in throttling the Russian. When Temple got to his feet, trembling, the Russian stared blankly at the ceiling. He would go on staring that way until someone shut his eyes.

Not questioning the incomprehensible, Temple knew he had done what he must. Hardly seeking for the motive he could not find he lifted the unconscious Sophia off the table, slung her long form across his shoulder, plodded with her from the room. Arkalion had said haste. He would hurry.

He next was aware of a spaceship. Remembering no time lag, he simply stood in the ship with Arkalion. And Sophia.

He knew it was a spaceship because he had been in one before and although the sensation of weightlessness was not present, they were in deep space. Stars you never see through an obscuring atmosphere hung suspended in the viewports. Cold-bright, not flickering against the plush blackness of deep space, phalanxes and legions of stars without numbers, in such wild profusion that space actually seemed three dimensional.

"This is a different sort of dream," said Sophia in English. "I remember. I remember everything. Kit—"

"Hello." He felt strangely shy, became mildly angry when Arkalion hardly tried to suppress a slight snicker. "Well, that second dream wasn't our idea," Temple protested. "Once there, we acted . . . and—"

"And . . ." said Sophia.

"And nothing," Arkalion told them. "You haven't time. This is a spaceship, not like the slow, bumbling craft your people use to reach Mars or Jupiter."

"Our people?" Temple demanded. "Not yours?"

"Will you let me finish? Light is a laggard crawler by comparison with the drive propelling this ship. Temple, Sophia, we are leaving your Galaxy altogether."

"Is that a fact" said Sophia, her Jupiter-found knowledge telling her they were traveling an unthinkable distance. "For some final contest between us, no doubt, to decide whether the U.S.S.R. or the U.S. represents Earth? Kit, I l-love you, but . . ."

"But Russia is more important, huh?"

"No. I didn't say that. All my training has been along those lines, though, and even if I'm aware it is indoctrination, the fact still remains. If your country is truly better, but if I have seen your country only through the eyes of Pravda, how can I . . . I don't know, Kit. Let me think."

"You needn't," said Arkalion, smiling. "If the two of you would let me get on with it you'd see this particular train of thought is meaningless, quite meaningless." Arkalion cleared his throat.

"Strange, but I have much the same problem as Sophia has. My indoctrination was far more subtle though. Far more convincing, based upon eons of propaganda methods. Temple, Sophia, those who initiated the Nowhere Journey for hundreds of worlds of your galaxy did so with a purpose."

"I know. To decide who gets their vast knowledge."

"Wrong. To find suitable hosts in a one-way relationship which is hardly symbiosis, really out and out parasitism."

"What?"

And Sophia: "What are you talking about?"

"The sick, decadent, tired old creatures you consider your superiors. Parasites. They need hosts in order to survive. Their old hosts have been milked dry, have become too highly specialized, are now incapable physically or emotionally of meeting a wide variety of environmental challenges. The Nowhere Journey is to find a suitable new host. They have found one. You of Earth."

"I don't understand," Temple said, remembering the glowing accounts of the 'superboys' he had been given by his brother Jason. "I just don't get it How can we be duped like that? Wouldn't someone have figured it out? And if they have all the power everyone says, there isn't much we can do about it, anyway."

Arkalion scowled darkly. "Then write Earth's obituary. You'll need one."

"Go ahead," Sophia told Arkalion. "There's more you want to say."

"All right. Temple's thought is correct. They have tremendous power. That is why you could be duped so readily. But their power is not concentrated here. These much-faster-than-light ships are an extreme rarity, for the power-drive no longer exists. Five ships in all, I believe. Hardly e-nough to invade a planet, even for them. It takes them thousands of years to get here otherwise. Thousands. Just as it took me, when I came to Mars and Earth in the first place."

"What?" cried Temple. "You . . ."

"I am one of them. Correct. I suppose you would call me a subversive, but I have made up my mind. Parasitism is unsatisfactory, when the Maker got us started on symbiosis.

Somewhere along the line, evolution took a wrong turn. We are—monsters."

"What do you look like?" Sophia demanded while Temple stood there shaking his head and muttering to himself.

"You couldn't see me, I am afraid. I was the representative here to see how things were going, and when my people found you of the Earth divided yourselves into two camps they realized they had been considering your abilities in halves. Put together, you are probably the top culture of your galaxy."

"So, we win," said Temple.

"Right and wrong. You lose. Earthmen will become hosts. Know what a back-seat driver is, Temple? You would be a back seat driver in your own body. Thinking, feeling, wanting to make decisions, but unable to. Eating when the parasite wants to, sleeping at his command, fighting, loving, living as he wills it. And perishing when he wants a new garment. Oh, they offer something in return. Their culture, their way of life, their scientific, economic, social system. It's good, too. But not worth it. Did you know that their economic struggle between democratic capitalism and totalitarian communism ended almost half a million years ago? What they have now is a system you couldn't even understand."

"Well," Temple mused, "even if everything you said were true—"

"Don't tell me you don't believe me?"

"If it were true and we wanted to do something about it, what could we do?"

"Now, nothing. Nothing but delay things by striking swiftly and letting fifty centuries of time perform your rearguard action. Destroy the one means your enemy has of reaching Earth within foreseeable time and you have destroyed his power to invade for a hundred centuries. He can still reach Earth, but the same way you journeyed to Nowhere. Ten thousand years of space travel in suspended animation. You saw me that way once, Temple, and wondered. You thought I was dead, but that is another story.

"Anyway, let my people invade your planet, ten thousand years hence. If Earth takes the right direction, if democracy and free thought and individual enterprise win over totalitarian standardization as I think they will, your people will be more than a match for the decadent parasites who may or may not have sufficient initiative to cross space the slow way and attempt invasion in ten thousand years."

"Ten thousand?" said Temple.

"Five from Earth to Nowhere. The distance to my home is far greater, but the rate of travel can be increased. Ten thousand years."

"Tell me," Temple demanded abruptly, "is this a dream?"

Arkalion smiled. "Yes and no. It is not a dream like the others because I assure you your bodies are not now resting on a pair of identical white tables. Still in the other dreams physical things could happen to you, while now you'll find you can do things as in a dream. For example, neither one of you knows the intricacies of a spaceship, yet if you are to save your planet, you must know the operation of the most intricate of all space ships, a giant space station."

"Then we're not dreaming?" asked Temple.

"I never said that. Consider this sequence of events about half way between the dream stage you have already seen and reality itself. Remember this: you'll have to work together; you'll have to function like machines. You will be handling totally alien equipment with only the sort of knowledge which can be played into your brains to guide you."

Sophia sighed. "Being an American, Kit is too much of an individual to help in such a situation."

Temple snorted. "Being a cog in a simple, state-wide machine is one thing—orienting yourself in a totally new situation is another."

"Yes, well—"

"See?" Arkalion cautioned. "See? Already you are arguing, but you must work together completely, with not the slightest conflict between you. As it is, you hardly have a chance."

"What about you?" said Sophia practically. "Can't you help?"

Arkalion shook his head. "No. While I'd like to see you come out of this thing on top, I would not like to sacrifice my life for it—which is exactly what I'd do if I remained with you and you lost.

"So, let's get down to detail. Imagine space being folded, imagine your time sense slowing, imagine a new dimension which negates the need for extensive linear travel, imagine anything you want—but we are in the process of moving nine hundred thousand light years through deep space. There is a great galaxy at that distance, almost a twin of your Milky Way: you call it the Andromeda Nebula. Closer to your own system are the two Magellanic Clouds, so called, something else which you table NGC 6822, and finally the Triangulum Galaxy. All have billions of stars, but none of the stars have life. To find life outside your galaxy you must seek it across almost a million light years. My people live in Andromeda.

"Guarding the flank of their galaxy and speeding through inter-galactic space at many light years per minute is what you might call a space station—but on a scale you've never dreamed of. Five of your miles in diameter, it is a fortress of terrible strength, a storehouse of half a million years of weapon development. It has been arranged that the one man running this station—"

"Just one?" Temple asked.

"Yes. You will see why when you get there. It has been arranged that he will leave, ostensibly on a scouting expedition. You see, I am not alone in this venture. At any rate, he will report that the space station has been taken—

as, indeed, it will be, by the two of you. The only ships capable of overtaking your station in its flight will be the only ships capable of reaching your galaxy before cultural development gives you a chance to survive. They will attack you. You will destroy them—or be destroyed yourselves. Any questions?"

The whole thing sounded fantastic to Temple. Could the fate of all Earth rest on their shoulders in a totally alien environment? Could they be expected to win? Temple had no reason to doubt the former, as wild as it sounded. As for the latter, all he could do was hope. "Tell me," he said, "how will we learn the use of all the weapons you claim are at our disposal?"

"Can you answer that for him, Sophia?" Arkalion wanted to know.

"Umm, I think so. The same way I had all sorts of culture crammed into me on Jupiter."

"Precisely. Only take it from me our refinement is far better, and the amount you have to learn actually is less."

"What I'd like to know—" Sophia began.

"Forget it. I want some sleep and you'll learn everything that's necessary at the space station."

And after that, ply Arkalion as they would with questions, he slumped down in his chair and rested. Temple could suddenly understand and appreciate. He felt like curling up into a tight little ball himself and sleeping until everything was over, one way or the other.

CHAPTER X

"IT'S ALL SO BIG! So incredible! We'll never understand it! Never . . ."

"Relax, Sophia. Arkalion said—"

"I know what Arkalion said, but we haven't learned anything yet."

Hours before, Arkalion had landed them on the space station, a gleaming, five-mile in diameter globe, and had quickly departed. Soon after that they had found themselves in a veritable labyrinth of tunnels, passageways, vaults. Occasionally they passed a great glowing screen, and always the view of space was the same. Like a magnificent, elongated shield, sparkling with a million million points of light, pale gold, burnished copper, blue of glacial ice and silver white, the Andromeda Galaxy spanned space from upper right to lower left. Off at the lower right hand corner they could see their space station; apparently the viewer itself stood far removed in space, projecting its images here at the globe.

Awed the first time they had seen one of the screens, Temple said, "All the poets who ever wrote a line would have given half their lives to see this as we see it now."

"And all the writers, musicians, artists . . ."

"Anyone who ever thought creatively, Sophia. How can you say it's breathtaking or anything like that when words weren't ever spoken which can . . ."

"Let's not go poetic just yet," Sophia admonished him with a smile. "We'd better get squared away here, as the expression goes, before it's too late."

"Yes . . . Hello, what's this?" A door irised open for them in a solid wall of metal. Irised was the only word Temple could think of, for a tiny round hole appeared in the wall spreading evenly in all directions with a slow, uniform, almost liquid motion. When it was large enough to walk through, they entered a completely bare room and Temple whirled in time to see the entrance irising shut.

"Something smells," said Sophia, sniffing at the air.

Sweet and cloying, the odor grew stronger. Temple may have heard a faint hissing sound. "I'm getting sleepy," he said.

Nodding, Sophia ran, banged on the wall where the door had opened so suddenly, then closed. No response. "Is it a trap?"

"By whom? For what?" Temple found it difficult to keep his eyes from closing. "Fight it if you want, Sophia. I'm going to sleep." And he squatted in the center of the floor, staring vacantly at the bare wall.

Just as Temple was drifting off into a dream about complex machinery he did not yet understand but realized he soon would, Sophia joined him the hard way, collapsing alongside of him, unconscious and sprawling gracelessly on the floor.

Temple slept.

"Sleepy-head, get up." Sophia stirred as he spoke and shook her. She yawned, stretched, smiled up at him lazily. "How do you feel now?"

"Hungry, Kit."

"That's a point. It's all right now, though. I know exactly where the food concentrates are kept. Three levels below us, second segment of the wall. You can make those queer doors iris by pressing the wall twice, with about a one second interval."

They found the food compartment, discovered row on row of cans, boxes, jars. Temple opened one of the cans, gazed in disappointment on a sorry looking thing the size of his thumb. Brown, shriveled, dry and almost flaky, it might have been a bird.

Sophia turned up her nose. "If that's the best this place has to offer, I'm not so hungry anymore."

Suddenly, she gaped. So did Temple. A savory odor attracted their attention, steam rising from the small can added to their interest. Amazing things happened to the withered scrap of food on exposure to the air. Temple barely had time to extract it from the can, burning his fingers in the process, when it became twice the can's size. It grew and by the time it finished, it was as savory looking a five pound fowl as Temple had ever seen. Roasted, steaming hot, ready to eat.

They tore into it with savage gusto.

"Stephanie should see me now," Temple found himself saying and regretted it.

"Stephanie? Who's that?"

"A girl."

"Your girl?"

· "What's the difference. She's a million light years and fifty centuries away."

"Answer me."

"Yes," said Temple, wishing he could change the subject. "My girl." He hadn't thought of Stephanie in a long time, perhaps because it was meaningless to think of someone dead fifty centuries. Now that the thoughts had been stirred within him, though, he found them poignantly pleasant.

"Your girl . . . and you would marry her if you could?"

He had grown attached to Sophia, not in reality, but in the second of their dream worlds. He wished the memory of the dream had not lingered for it disturbed him. In it he had loved Sophia as much as he now loved Stephanie although the one was obtainable and the other was a five-thousand year pinch of dust. And how much of the dream lingered with him, in his head and his heart?

"Let's forget about it," Temple suggested.

"No. If she were here today and if everything were normal, would you marry her?"

"Why talk about what can't be?"

"I want to know, that's why."

"All right. Yes, I would. I would marry Stephanie."

"Oh," said Sophia. "Then what happened in the dream meant . . . nothing."

"We were two different people," Temple said coolly, then wished he hadn't for it was only half-true. He remembered everything about the dream-which-was-more-than-a-dream vividly. He had been far more intimate with Sophia, and over a longer period of time, than he had ever been with Stephanie. And even if Stephanie appeared impossibly on the spot and he spent the rest of his life as her husband, still he would never forget his dream-life with Sophia. In time he could let himself tell her that. But not now; now the best thing he could do would be to change the subject.

"I see," Sophia answered him coldly.

"No, you don't. Maybe some day you will."

"There's nothing but what you old me. I see."

"No . . . forget it," he told her wearily.

"Of course. It was only a dream anyway. The dream before that I almost killed you out of hatred anyway. Love and hate, I guess they neutralize. We're just a couple of people who have to do a job together, that's all."

"For gosh sakes, Sophia! That isn't true. I loved Stephanie. I still would, were Stephanie alive. But she's—she's about as accessible as the Queen of Sheba."

"So? There's an American expression—you're carrying a torch."

Probably, Temple realized, it was true. But what did all of that have to do with Sophia? If he and Sophia . . . if they . . . would it be fair to Sophia? It would be exactly as if a widower remarried, with the memory of his first wife set aside in his heart . . . no, different, for he had never wed

Stephanie, and always in him would be the desire for what had never been.

"Let's talk about it some other time," Temple almost pleaded, wanting the respite for himself as much as for Sophia.

"No. We don't have to talk about it ever. I won't be second best, Kit. Let's forget all about it and do our job. I—I'm sorry I brought the whole thing up."

Temple felt like an unspeakable heel. And, anyway, the whole thing wasn't resolved in his mind. But they couldn't just let it go at that, not in case something happened when the ships came and one or both of them perished. Awkwardly, for now he felt self-conscious about everything, he got his arms about Sophia, drew her to him, placed his lips to hers.

That was as far as he got. She wrenched free, shoved clear of him. "If you try that again, you will have another dislocated jaw."

Temple shrugged wearily. If anything were to be resolved between them, it would be later.

When the ships came moments afterwards—seven, not the five Arkalion predicted—they were completely unprepared.

Temple spotted them first on one of the viewing screens, half way between the receiver and the space station itself, silhouetted against the elongated shield of Andromeda. They soared out of the picture, appeared again minutes later, zooming in from the other direction in two flights of four ships and three.

"Come on!" Sophia cried over her shoulder, irising the door and plunging from the room. Temple followed at her heels but her Jupiter trained muscles pushed her lithe legs in long, powerful strides and soon she outdistanced him. By the time he reached the armaments vault, breathless, she was seated at the single gun-emplacement, her fingers on the controls.

"Watch the viewing screen and tell me how we're doing,"

Sophia told him, not taking her eyes from the dials and levers.

Temple watched, fascinated, saw a thin pencil of radiant energy leap out into space, missing one of the ships by what looked like a scant few miles. He called the corrective azimuth to her, hardly surprised by the way his mind had absorbed and now could use its new-found knowledge.

Temple understood and yet did not understand. For example, he knew the station had but one gun and Sophia sat at it now, yet in certain ways it didn't make sense. Could it cover all sectors of space? His mind supplied the answer although he had not been aware of the knowledge an instant before: yes. The space station did not merely rotate. Its surface was a spherical projection of a moving Moebius strip and although he tried to envision the concept, he failed. The weapon could be fired at any given point in space at twenty second intervals, covering every other conceivable point in the ensuing time.

Sophia was firing again and Temple watched the thin beam leap across space. "Hit!" he roared. "Hit!"

Something flashed at the front end of the lead ship. The light blinded him, but when he could see again only six ships remained in space—casting perfect shadows on the Andromeda Galaxy! The source of light, Temple realized triumphantly, was out of range, but he could picture it—a glowing derelict of a ship, spewing heat, light and radioactivity into the void.

"One down," Sophia called. "Six to go. I like your American expressions. Like sitting ducks—"

She did not finish. Abruptly, light flared all around them. Something shrieked in Temple's ears. The vault shuddered, shook. Girders clattered to the floor, stove it in, revealing black rock. Sophia was thrown back from the single gun, crashing against the wall, flipping in air and landing on her stomach.

Temple ran to her, turned her over. Blood smeared her face, trickled from her lips. Although she did not move, she wasn't dead. Temple half dragged, half carried her from the vault into an adjoining room. He stretched her out comfortably as he could on the floor, ran back into the vault.

Molten metal had collected in one corner of the room, crept sluggishly toward him across the floor, heating it white-hot. He skirted it, climbed over a twisted girder, pushed his way past other debris, found himself at the gun emplacement.

"How dumb can I get?" Temple said aloud. "Sophia ran to the gun, must have assumed I set up the shields." Again, it was an item of information stored in his mind by the wisdom of the space station. Protective shields made it impossible for anything but a direct hit on the emplacement to do them any harm, only Temple had never set the shields in place. He did so now, merely by tripping a series of levers, but glancing at a dial to his left he realized with alarm that the damage possibly had already been done. The needle, which measured lethal radiation, hovered half way between negative and the critical area marked in red and, even as Temple watched it, crept closer to the red.

How much time did he have? Temple could not be sure, bent grimly over the weapon. It was completely unfamiliar to his mind, completely unfamiliar to his fingers. He toyed with it, released a blast of radiant energy, whirled to face the viewing screen. The beam streaked out into the void, clearly hundreds of miles from its objective.

Cursing, Temple tried again, scoring a near miss. The ships were trading a steady stream of fire with him now, but with the shielding up it was harmless, striking and then bouncing back into space. Temple scored his first hit five minutes after sitting down at the gun, whooped triumphantly and fired again. Five ships left.

But the dial indicated an increase in radioactivity as newly created neutrons spread their poison like a cancer. Behind Temple, the vault was a shambles. The pool of molten metal had increased in size, almost cutting off any possibility of escape. He could jump it now, Temple realized, but it might grow larger. Consolidating its gains now, it had sheared a pit in the floor, had commenced vaporizing the rock below it, hissing and lapping with white-hot insistence.

Something boomed, grated, booned again and Temple watched another girder bounce off the floor, dip one end into the molten pool and clatter out a stub. Apparently the damage was extensive; a structural weakness threatened to make the entire ceiling go.

Temple fired again, got another ship. He could almost feel death breathing on his shoulder, in no great hurry but sure of its prize. He fired the weapon.

If one ship remained when they could no longer use the gun, they would have failed. One ship might make the difference for Earth. One . . .

Three left. Two.

They raked the space station with blast after blast—futilely. They spun and twisted and streaked by, offering poor targets. Temple waited his chance . . . and glanced at the dial which measured radioactivity. He yelped, stood up. The needle had encroached upon the red area. Death to remain where he was more than a moment or two. Not quick death, but rather slow and lingering. He could do what he had to, then perish hours later. His life—for Earth? If Arkalion had known all the answers, and if he could get both ships and if there weren't another alternative for the aliens, the parasites . . . Temple stabbed out with his pencil beam, caught the sixth ship, then saw the needle dip completely into the red. He got up trembling, stepped back, half tripped on the stump of a girder as his eyes strayed in fascination to the viewing screen. The seventh ship was out of range, hovering off in the void somewhere, awaiting its chance. If Temple left the gun the ship would come in close enough to hit the emplacement despite its protective shielding. Well, it was suicide to remain there—especially when the ship wasn't even in view.

Temple leaped over the molten pool and left the vault.

He found Sophia stirring, sitting up.

"What hit me?" she said, and laughed. "Something seems to have gone wrong, Kit . . . what . . . ?"

"It's all right now," he told her, lying.

"You look pale."

"You got one. I got five. One ship to go."

"What are you waiting for?" And Sophia sprang to her feet, heading for the vault.

"Hold it!" Temple snapped. "Don't go in there."

"Why not. I'll get the last ship and—"

"*Don't go in there!*" Temple tugged at her arm, pulled her away from the vault and its broken door which would not iris closed any more.

"What's the matter, Kit?"

"I—I want to finish the last one myself, that's all."

Sophia got herself loose, reached the circular doorway, peered inside. "Like Dante's Inferno," she said. "You told me nothing was the matter. Well, we can get through to the emplacement, Kit."

"No." And again he stopped her. At least he had lived in freedom all his life and although he was still young and did not want to die, Sophia had never known freedom until now and it wouldn't be right if she perished without savoring its fruits. He had a love, dust fifty centuries, he had his past and his memories. Sophia had only the future. Clearly, if someone had to yield life, Temple would do it.

"It's worse than it looks," he told her quietly, drawing her back from the door again. He explained what had happened, told her the radioactivity had not quite reached critical point—which was a lie. "No," he concluded, "we're wasting time. If I rush in there, fire, and rush right out everything will be fine."

"Then let me. I'm quicker than you."

"No. I—I'm more familiar with the gun." Dying would not be too bad, if he went with reasonable certainty he had saved the Earth. No man ever died so importantly, Temple thought briefly, then felt cold fear when he realized it would be dying just the same. He fought it down, said: "I'll be right back."

Sophia looked at him, smiling vaguely. "Then you insist on doing it?"

When he nodded she told him, "Then,—kiss me. Kiss me now, Kit—in case something . . ."

Fiercely, he swept her to him, bruising her lips with his. "Sophia, Sophia . . ."

At last, she drew back. "Kit," she said, smiling demurely. She took his right hand in her left, held it, squeezed it. Her own right hand she suddenly brought up from her waist, fist clenched, driving it against his jaw.

Temple fell, half stunned by the blow, at her feet. For the space of a single heartbeat he watched her move slowly toward the round doorway, then he had clambered to his feet, running after her. He got his arms on her shoulders, yanked at her.

When she turned he saw she was crying. "I—I'm sorry, Kit. You couldn't fool me about . . . Stephanie. You can't fool me about this." She had more leverage this time. She stepped back, bringing her small, hard fist up from her knees. It struck Temple squarely at the point of the jaw, with the strength of Jovian-trained muscle behind it. Temple's feet left the floor and he landed with a thud on his back. His last thought of Sophia—or of anything, for a while—made him smile faintly as he lost consciousness. For a kiss she had promised him another dislocated jaw, and she had kept her promise . . ."

Later, how much later he did not know, something soft cushioned his head. He opened his eyes, stared through swirling, spinning murk. He focused, saw Arkalion. No—*two* Arkalions standing off at a distance, watching him. He squirmed, knew his head was cushioned in a woman's lap. He sighed, tried to sit up and failed. Soft hands caressed his forehead, his cheeks. A face swam into vision, but mistily. "Sophia," he murmured. His vision cleared.

It was Stephanie.

"It's over," said Arkalion.

"We're on our way back to Earth, Kit."

"But the ships—"

"All destroyed. If my people want to come here in ten thousand years, let them try. I have a hunch you of Earth will be ready for them."

"It took us five thousand to reach Nowhere," Temple mused. "It will take us five thousand to return. We'll come barely in time to warn Earth—"

"Wrong," said Arkalion. "I still have my ship. We're in it now, so you'll reach Earth with almost fifty centuries to spare. Why don't you forget about it, though? If human progress for the next five thousand years matches what has been happening for the last five, the parasites won't stand a chance."

"Earth—five thousand years in the future," Stephanie said dreamily. "I wonder what it will be like . . . Don't be so startled, Kit. I was a pilot study on the Nowhere Journey. If I made it successfully, other women would have been sent. But now there won't be any need."

"I wouldn't be too sure of that," said the real Alaric Arkalion III. "I suspect a lot of people are going to feel just like me. Why not go out and colonize space. We can do it. Wonderful to have a frontier again . . . Why, a dozen billionaires will appear for every one like my father. Good for the economy."

"So, if we don't like Earth," said Stephanie, "we can always go out."

"I have a strong suspicion you will like it," said Arkalion's double.

Alaric III grinned. "What about you, bud? I don't want a twin brother hanging around all the time."

Arkalion grinned back at him. "What do you want me to do, young man? I've forsaken my people. This is now my body. Tell you what, I promise to be always on a different continent. Earth isn't so small that I'll get in your hair."

Temple sat up, felt the bandages on his jaw. He smiled at Stephanie, told her he loved her and meant it. It was exactly as if she had returned from the grave and in his first exultation he hadn't even thought of Sophia, who had perished all alone in the depths of space that a world might live . . .

He turned to Arkalion. "Sophia?"

"We found her dead, Kit. But smiling, as if everything was worth it."

"It should have been me."

"Whoever Sophia was," said Stephanie, "she must have been a wonderful woman, because when you got up, when you came to, her name was . . ."

"Forget it," said Temple. "Sophia and I have a very strange relationship and . . ."

"All right, you said forget it. Forget it." Stephanie smiled down at him. "I love you so much there isn't even room for jealousy . . . Ummm . . . Kit . . ."

"Break up that clinch," ordered Arkalion "We're making one more stop at Nowhere to pick up anyone who wants to return to Earth. Some of 'em probably won't but those who do are welcome . . ."

"Jason will stay," Temple predicted. "He'll be a leader out among the stars."

"Then he'll have to climb over my back," Alaric III predicted happily, his eyes on the viewport hungrily.

Temple's jaw throbbed. He was tired and sleepy. But satisfied. Sophia had died and for that he was sad, but there would always be a place deep in his heart for the memory of her: delicious, somehow exotic, not a love the way Stephanie was, not as tender, not as sure . . . but a feeling for Sophia that was completely unique. And whenever the strangeness of the far-future Earth frightened Temple, whenever he felt a situation might get the better of him, whenever doubt clouded judgment, he would remember the tall lithe girl who had walked to her death that a world might have the freedom she barely had tasted. And together with Stephanie he would be able to do anything.

Unless, he thought dreamily as he drifted off to sleep, his head pillowed again on Stephanie's lap, he'd wind up with a bum jaw the rest of his life.

www.ingramcontent.com/pod-product-compliance
Lightning Source LLC
Chambersburg PA
CBHW050803250626
47155CB00005B/2190